BRI

WINTER

Whether it's getting through heavy traffic, facing an illness, living in a rough neighborhood or having to deal with a northern winter as Brian does makes no matter, the art of survival is the same —it is bad and you use your brain and body to get through it. The tools for survival are in all of us, just waiting to be used . . .

Gary Paulsen

BRIAN'S WINTER

GARY PAULSEN

SCHOLASTIC INC.
New York Toronto London Auckland Sydney

ISBN 0-590-69013-2

12 11 10 9 8 7 6 5 4 3 2 1   8 9/9 0 1 2 3/0

Printed in the U.S.A.   40

First Scholastic printing, January 1998

For Caitlin, Matt and Nick Spille

BRIAN'S WINTER

FOREWORD

This book was written for all those readers of *Hatchet* and *The River* who wrote (I received as many as two hundred letters a day) to tell me they felt Brian Robeson's story was left unfinished by his early rescue before, they said, "it became really hard going." They asked: "What would happen if Brian hadn't been rescued, if he had had to survive in the winter?" Since my life has been one of survival in winter—running two Iditarods, hunting and trapping as a boy and young man—the challenge became interesting, and so I researched and wrote *Brian's Winter*, showing what could and perhaps would have happened had Brian not been rescued.

For the purpose of this story it is necessary to shift the idea left by *Hatchet* and suppose that although Brian did retrieve the survival pack from the plane, he did not trigger a radio signal and did not get rescued. Other than that I hope I have remained true to the story in *Hatchet* and that this book will answer the question of Brian's winter survival.

It is important to note, however, that his previous knowledge was vital—he had to know summer survival to attempt living in winter. Had he been dropped in the winter with no previous knowledge of hunting, surviving, no education gained in the school of hard knocks during the summer, Brian probably would have died no matter what his luck or abilities.

Part One

FALL

ONE

Fall came on with a softness, so that Brian didn't realize what was in store—a hard-spined north woods winter—until it was nearly too late.

He had never thought he would be here this long. After the plane crash that marooned him in the wilderness he had lived day by day for fifty-four days, until he had found the survival pack in the plane. Then another thirty-five days through the northern summer, somehow living the same day-to-day pattern he had started just after the crash.

To be sure he was very busy. The emergency pack on the plane had given him a gun with fifty shells—a survival .22 rifle—a hunting knife with a compass in the handle, cooking pots and pans, a fork, spoon and knife, matches, two butane lighters, a sleeping bag and foam pad, a first-aid kit with scissors, a cap that said CESSNA, fishing line, lures, hooks and sinkers, and several packets of freeze-dried food. He tried to ration the food out but found it impossible, and within two weeks he had eaten it all, even the package of dried prunes—something he'd hated in his old life. They tasted like candy and were so good he ate the whole package in one sitting. The results were nearly as bad as when he'd glutted on the gut cherries when he first landed. His stomach tied in a knot and he spent more than an hour at his latrine hole.

In truth he felt relieved when the food was gone. It had softened him, made him want more and more, and he could tell that he was moving mentally away from the woods, his situation. He started to think in terms of the city again, of hamburgers and malts, and his dreams changed.

In the days, weeks and months since the plane had crashed he had dreamed many times. At first all the dreams had been of food—food he had eaten, food he wished he had eaten and food he wanted to eat. But as time progressed the food dreams seemed to phase out and he dreamed of other things—of friends, of his parents (always of their worry, how they wanted to see him; sometimes that they were back together) and more and more of girls. As with food he dreamed of girls he knew, girls he wished he had known and girls he wanted to know.

But with the supplies from the plane his dreams changed back to food and when it was gone—in what seemed a very short time—a kind of wanting hunger returned that he had not felt since the first week. For a week or two he was in torment, never satisfied; even when he had plenty of fish and rabbit or foolbird to eat he thought of the things he *didn't* have. It somehow was never enough and he seemed to be angry all the time, so angry that he wasted a whole day just slamming things around and swearing at his luck.

When it finally ended—wore away, was more like it—he felt a great sense of relief. It was as if somebody he didn't like had been visiting and had finally gone. It was then that he first really noted the cold.

Almost a whiff, something he could smell. He was hunting with the rifle when he sensed the change. He had awakened early, just before first light, and had decided to spend the entire day hunting and get maybe two or three foolbirds. He blew on the coals from the fire the night before until they glowed red, added some bits of dry grass, which burst into flame at once, and heated water in one of the aluminum pots that had come in the plane's survival pack.

"Coffee," he said, sipping the hot water. Not that he'd ever liked coffee, but something about having a hot liquid in the morning made the day easier to start—gave him time to think, plan his morning. As he sipped, the sun came up over the lake and for the hundredth time he noted how beautiful it was—mist rising, the new sun shining like gold.

He banked the fire carefully with dirt to keep the coals hot for later, picked up the rifle and moved into the woods.

He was, instantly, hunting.

All sounds, any movement went into him, filled his eyes, ears, mind so that he became part of it, and it was then that he noted the change.

A new coolness, a touch, a soft kiss on his cheek. It was the same air, the same sun, the same morning, but it was different, so changed that he stopped and raised his hand to his cheek and touched where the coolness had brushed him.

"Why is it different?" he whispered. "What smell . . ."

But it wasn't a smell so much as a feeling, a newness in the air, a chill. There and gone, a brush of new-cool air on his cheek, and he should have known what it meant but just then he saw a rabbit and raised the little rifle, pulled the trigger and heard only a click. He recocked the bolt, made certain there was a cartridge in the chamber and aimed again—the rabbit had remained sitting all this time—and pulled the trigger once more. *Click.*

He cleared the barrel and turned the rifle up to the dawn light. At first he couldn't see anything different. He had come to know the rifle well. Although he still didn't like it much—the noise of the small gun seemed terribly out of place and scared game away—he had to admit it made the shooting of game easier, quicker. He had a limited number of shells and realized they would not last forever, but he still had come to depend on the rifle. Finally, as he pulled the bolt back to get the light down in the action, he saw it.

The firing pin—a raised part of the bolt—was broken cleanly away. Worse, it could not be repaired without special tools, which he did not have. That made the rifle worthless, at least as far as being a gun was concerned, and he swore and started back to the camp to get his bow and arrows and in the movement of things completely ignored the warning nature had put on his cheek just before he tried to shoot the rabbit.

In camp he set the rifle aside—it might have some use later as a tool—and picked up the bow.

He had come to depend too much on the rifle and for a

moment the bow and handful of arrows felt unfamiliar to his hands. Before he was away from the camp he stopped and shot several times into a dirt hummock. The first shot went wide by two feet and he shook his head.

Focus, he thought, bring it back.

On the second shot he looked at the target, into the target, drew and held it for half a second—focusing all the while on the dirt hump—and when he released the arrow with a soft *thrum* he almost didn't need to watch it fly into the center of the lump. He knew where the arrow would go, knew before he released it, knew almost before he drew it back.

From my brain, he thought, from my brain through my arm into the bow and through the string to the arrow it must all be one, and it *is* all one.

Three more times he shot and the arrows drove into the center of the hummock and then he was satisfied.

He left the camp again, put the sleeve quiver made from his old windbreaker on his right shoulder and walked slowly, watching, listening until he saw the curve of the back of a rabbit near a small clump of hazel brush.

It was too far for a shot and he quickly averted his eyes and froze for a moment before moving closer. He'd learned much from the woods, from mistakes, and one thing he'd come to know was that game spooked if it "felt" that it was known. It was always better to look away, move sideways instead of directly toward it, and he worked now to the left, letting the brush cover his movement until he was no more than fifteen feet away from the rabbit.

He drew the bow, aimed for the center of the rabbit and released when he felt the arrow would fly right.

It took the rabbit almost exactly in the center of its chest and drove through cleanly, killing it almost instantly.

They were not all this clean, the kills, and he was grateful. He had not grown accustomed to killing in spite of how much of it he had done.

He had learned this: Nothing that lived, nothing that walked or crawled or flew or swam or slithered or oozed— nothing, not one thing on God's earth wanted to die. No matter what people thought or said about chickens or fish or cattle—they all wanted to live.

But Brian had become part of nature, had become a predator, a two-legged wolf. And there was a physics to it, a basic fact, almost a law: For a wolf to live, something else had to die. And for Brian to live it was the same. His body was a machine, it needed food, needed calories, and for that to happen something had to die. But sometimes it did not go well. Sometimes the arrow did not hit a vital place—did not hit the heart or lungs—and the rabbit or grouse died more slowly. The first time this had happened a kind of panic had taken him. He had shot a rabbit through the middle, the stomach, and it had tried to run and then had flopped around and he had shot the rabbit again and again, pounding arrows into the poor thing until it had at last died and when he'd cooked it and eaten it—as hunger forced him to do—the rabbit had tasted like wood and made him so sick he nearly threw up.

It was the only thing he had liked about the rifle. It

killed quickly, caused a kind of wound shock that stunned as it killed.

But he was once more with the bow now and the silence of it brought him back to being more a part of the woods and he moved easily as he carried the dead rabbit back to camp.

It was afternoon by the time he had the fire rekindled and had set to cleaning the rabbit. Much had changed since he had retrieved the survival pack from the plane. He had a hunting knife now, and that made cleaning game much easier and faster.

He still wasted nothing. He used the knife to split the rabbit down the middle of the belly and skinned it carefully and then gutted it, using the curve of the knife to clean out the cavity. The head and lungs and intestines and stomach and liver he set aside for fish bait and food, as well as the heart. Then he cut the body up into pieces, carving it at the joints, and put them in a pot with fresh lake water, which he set on the fire to boil. He had found it best to boil everything. Initially he had cooked meat over the fire on a stick—something he had seen in movies and on television—but it was the wrong way to cook. The flame heated the meat and all the juices—all the vitamins and nutrients—dripped into the fire. Everything was wasted. But by boiling the meat he made a stew and when he drank the juice-broth he not only had a rich soup but something to sip as well.

He leaned back against the rock wall next to his shelter opening and took a minute to think while the meat cooked. It amazed him how little time he had to do that—sit and think. It seemed the longer he was in the woods—he had marked sixty-eight days counting this day—the more there was to do. Firewood was an endless chore of course—he kept the fire going whenever he was there and banked it when he left. And since he had burned all the easy wood, the wood close to camp, it took longer to bring wood in. But that wasn't all of his life and it seemed that everything he had to do doubled.

He would get up, check his fishing lines, and remove any fish to store in his live-fish pool along the shore. Then see to airing out the sleeping bag and tend to his toilet and hunt for the day's meat and clean it (if he made a kill—he often did not) and cook it and stretch the hide (if it was a rabbit) to dry and eat and bank the fire for night and another day was gone . . .

Just stopping to sit and think was a rare thing. At first he didn't like it much because it brought memories and made him homesick, made him miss his mother and father and other life. But now he relished the time, and he spent it this day doing something he called "visiting." He would pick somebody back in what he thought of as "the world" and sit and have an imaginary chat with him or her. Usually it was his mother or father, sometimes a friend and once or twice a movie or rock star.

Initially he worried that he might be going crazy. But then he decided if you felt you were crazy you weren't really crazy because he had heard somewhere that crazy people didn't know they were insane. So he went ahead and had the visits.

He sat now and visited with his mother. By looking across the lake and letting his eyes go out of focus he could visualize her face, hear her laugh, and he sat chatting in his mind with her, asking how she was doing, telling her of his life now, and before long he was surprised to see that the meat had cooked.

Brian took the pot off the flame to cool and went down to check the fishing line. There was a small panfish on it—it had blue gills—and he took it off the hook and put it in the holding pen with the others. It was his only "saved" food, the little pool of fish, and no matter how small the fish, he kept them all. He had learned that as well—food was everything. Just everything. And none of it, not even the smallest fish, could be let go.

When he arrived back at the shelter the meat and broth had cooled and he ate quickly. Flies had come when he gutted the rabbit and they stayed for dinner while he ate. He brushed them away as he ate the meat from the bones and drank the broth, a full quart. They followed him as he went back to the lake to clean the pot and only left him when there wasn't a smell of food anywhere in the area.

He stacked wood for the night fire and made his bed by restacking the mattress of pine boughs and unrolling the sleeping bag and foam pad, and here he got another warning that he ignored. When he slid into the bag and turned so that he felt the heat from the fire on his face coming through the opening it did not feel uncomfortable. He snuggled down into the bag and felt glad for its warmth, and the thought that this was the first time he'd felt glad for heat this season—that it was growing colder—somehow eluded him.

He closed his eyes and went to sleep like a baby.

Chapter

TWO

For two weeks the weather grew warmer and each day was more glorious than the one before. Hunting seemed to get better as well. Brian took foolbirds or rabbits every day and on one single day he took three foolbirds.

He ate everything and felt fat and lazy and one afternoon he actually lay in the sun. It was perhaps wrong to say he was happy. He spent too much time in loneliness for true happiness. But he found himself smiling as he worked around the camp and actually looked forward to bringing in wood in the soft afternoons just because it kept him out rummaging around in the woods.

He had made many friends—or at least acquaintances. Birds had taken on a special significance for him. At night the owls made their soft sounds, calling each other in almost ghostly *hooonnes* that scared him until he finally saw one call on a night when the moon was full and so bright it was almost like a cloudy day. He slept with their calls and before long would awaken if they didn't call.

Before dawn, just as gray light began to filter through the trees, the day birds began to sing. They started slowly but before the gray had become light enough to see ten yards *all* the birds started to sing and Brian was brought out of sleep by what seemed to be thousands of singing birds.

At first it all seemed to be noise but as he learned and listened, he found them all to be different. Robins had an evening song and one they sang right before a rainstorm and another when the rain was done. Blue jays spent all their time complaining and swearing but they also warned him when something—anything—was moving in the woods. Ravens and crows were the same—scrawking and cawing their way through the trees.

It was all, Brian found, about territory. Everybody wanted to own a place to live, a place to hunt. Birds didn't sing for fun, they sang to warn other birds to keep away— sang to tell them to stay out of their territory.

He had learned about property from the wolves. Several times he had seen a solitary wolf—a large male that came near the camp and studied the boy. The wolf did not seem to be afraid and did nothing to frighten Brian, and Brian even thought of him as a kind of friend.

The wolf seemed to come on a regular schedule, hunting, and Brian guessed that he ran a kind of circuit. At night while gazing at the fire Brian figured that if the wolf made five miles an hour and hunted ten hours a day, he must be traveling close to a hundred-mile loop.

After a month or so the wolf brought a friend, a smaller, younger male, and the second time they both came they stopped near Brian's camp and while Brian watched they peed on a rotten stump, both going twice on the same spot.

Brian had read about wolves and seen films about them and knew that they "left sign," using urine to mark their territory. He had also read—he thought in a book by Farley Mowat—that the wolves respected others' territories as well as their own. As soon as they were well away from the old stump Brian went up and peed where they had left sign.

Five days later when they came through again Brian saw them stop, smell where he had gone and then spot the ground next to Brian's spot, accepting his boundary.

Good, he thought. I own something now. I belong. And he had gone on with his life believing that the wolves and he had settled everything.

But wolf rules and Brian rules only applied to wolves and Brian.

Then the bear came.

Brian had come to know bears as well as he knew wolves or birds. They were usually alone—unless it was a female with cubs—and they were absolutely, totally devoted to eating. He had seen them several times while picking berries, raking the bushes with their teeth to pull the fruit off—and a goodly number of leaves as well, which they spit out before swallowing the berries—and, as with the wolves, they seemed to get along with him.

That is to say Brian would see them eating and he would move away and let them pick where they wanted while he found another location. It worked for the bears, he thought, smiling, and it worked for him, and this thinking evolved into what Brian thought of as an understanding between him and the bears: Since he left them alone, they would leave him alone.

Unfortunately the bears did not know that it was an agreement, and Brian was suffering under the misunderstanding that, as in some imaginary politically correct society, everything was working out.

All of this made him totally unprepared for the reality of the woods. To wit: Bears and wolves did what they wanted to do, and Brian had to fit in.

He was literally awakened to the facts one morning during the two-week warm spell. Brian had been sleeping soundly and woke to the clunking sound of metal on rock. His mind and ears were tuned to all the natural sounds around him and there was no sound in nature of metal on stone. It snapped him awake in midbreath.

He was sleeping with his head in the opening of the shelter and he had his face out and when he opened his eyes he saw what appeared to be a wall of black-brown fur directly in front of him.

He thought he might be dreaming and shook his head but it didn't go away and he realized in the same moment that he was looking at the rear end of a bear. No, he thought with a clinical logic that surprised him—I am looking at the very *large* rear end of a very *large* bear.

The bear had come to Brian's camp—smelling the gut-smell of the dead rabbit, and the cooking odor from the pot. The bear did not see it as Brian's camp or territory. There was a food smell, it was hungry, it was time to eat.

It had found the pot and knife by the fire where Brian

18

had left them and scooped them outside. Brian had washed them both in the lake when he finished eating, but the smell of food was still in the air. Working around the side of the opening, the bear had bumped the pan against a rock at the same moment that it had settled its rump in the entrance of Brian's shelter.

Brian pulled back a foot. "Hey—get out of there!" he yelled, and kicked the bear in the rear.

He was not certain what he expected. Perhaps that the bear would turn and realize its mistake and then sheepishly trundle away. Or that the bear would just run off.

With no hesitation, not even the smallest part of a second's delay, the bear turned and ripped the entire log side off the shelter with one sweep of a front paw and a moist *"whouuuff"* out of its nostrils.

Brian found himself looking up at the bear, turned now to look down on the boy, and with another snort the bear swung its left paw again and scooped Brian out of the hollow of the rock and flung him end over end for twenty feet. Then the bear slipped forward and used both front paws to pack Brian in a kind of ball and whap him down to the edge of the water, where he lay, dazed, thinking in some way that he was still back in the shelter.

The bear stopped and studied Brian for a long minute, then turned back to ransacking the camp, looking for where that delicious smell had come from. It sat back on its haunches and felt the air with its nostrils, located another faint odor stream and followed it down to the edge of the water where the fish pool lay. It dug in the water—

not more than ten feet from where Brian now lay, trying to figure out if his arms and legs were still all attached to where they had been before—and pulled up the rabbit skull, still with bits of meat on it, and swallowed it whole. It dug around in the water again and found the guts and ate them and went back to rummaging around in the pool, and when nothing more could be found the bear looked once more at Brian, at the camp, and then walked away without looking back.

Other than some minor scratches where the bear's claws had slightly scraped him—it was more a boxing action than a clawing one—Brian was in one piece. He was still jolted and confused about just exactly which end was up, but most of all he was grateful.

He knew that the bear could have done much more damage than it had. He had seen a bear tear a stump out of the ground like a giant tooth when it was looking for grubworms and ants. This bear could just as easily have killed him, and had actually held back.

But as the day progressed Brian found himself stiffening, and by the time he was ready for bed his whole body ached and he knew he would be covered with bruises from the encounter.

He would have to find some way to protect himself, some weapon. The fire worked well when it was burning, but it had burned down. His hatchet and knife would have done nothing more than make the bear really angry—something he did not like to think about—and his bow was good only for smaller game. He had never tried to shoot anything bigger than a foolbird or rabbit with it and doubted that the bow would push the arrow deep enough to do anything but—again—make the bear really mad.

He bundled in his bag that night, the end of the two weeks of warm weather. He kept putting wood on the fire, half afraid the bear would come back. All the while he tried to think of a solution.

But in reality, the bear was not his primary adversary. Nor was the wolf, nor any animal. Brian had become his own worst enemy because in all the business of hunting, fishing and surviving he had forgotten the primary rule: Always, *always* pay attention to what was happening. Everything in nature means something and he had missed the warnings that summer was ending, had in many ways already ended, and what was coming would be the most dangerous thing he had faced since the plane crash.

Chapter

THREE

He decided he needed a stronger weapon, a larger bow. He thought of it as a war bow. He would need arrows tipped with some kind of sharpened head. He had been hunting with wood arrows with fire-hardened tips but all they did was make a hole; they didn't provide any cutting action, which he felt would work best with a stronger bow.

He used a hardwood tree he found by the lake. It had straight branches with a slickish gray bark and seemed to have a snap to it that other woods didn't hold. He spent one whole day cutting a long, straight piece of wood and skinning and shaping it with the hunting knife and his hatchet into a bow shape slightly longer than he was tall. He did not hurry but kept at it with a steady pace and by dark the bow was ready to dry.

Arrow shafts took two days in the sun to dry once they were stripped of their bark, and he thought the bow might take four or five. He took time to cut another straight limb and shape another bow, working by firelight into the night. It wouldn't hurt to have two bows and if one broke he had a backup.

He had not hunted for three days now but had eaten well of foolbird and rabbit on his last hunt and he took time to take two fish from the pool and cook them before going to sleep, boiling them into a fish soup, which he drank-spooned-fingerpicked until the bones were clean.

That night it was cold. Cold enough so that the sleeping bag felt almost delicious, and just as he closed his eyes it came to him—all the signs, all the little nudges. The cold would get worse. Summer was over. He would not get rescued—he had finally given up on it and no longer listened or looked for planes—and he was going to get hit with a northern winter.

All of that came to him just as he started to doze and it snapped him awake and kept him awake until exhaustion finally made him sleep.

In the morning he awakened with the same feeling of urgency and spent the day cutting arrow shafts from the willows for his war bow and trying to reason out what he needed to do to get ready for the coming winter.

He had no warm clothing or footgear. The sleeping bag was a good one, though not a true winter bag. It was effective to perhaps twenty above, if used in a good shelter. But that was all he had, the sleeping bag, and he couldn't spend all his time just lying in the bag. He would starve and die. He would have to continue hunting, eating, living.

He looked at the shelter with new eyes. He had repaired the damage the bear had done. He studied his home while stripping the bark from the two dozen arrow shafts he'd cut for the war bow.

Three sides were of rock and they were snug. But the

side he had filled in with logs and limbs and branches was far from airtight—he could see through it in several places—and would have to be winterized. He could pack it with dead leaves or even cut strips of sod with the hatchet to fill it in. And make an insulated door by stuffing two woven frames full of leaves. The problem—well, he thought, smiling, one of about a thousand problems—was that he didn't honestly know how cold it would get or how much snow there would be or what he could do to live. What would be available to hunt in the winter? He knew some things migrated but he wasn't sure which things or if even rabbits came out—maybe they stayed inside brushpiles or caves all winter and slept. Also, would he have to have a fire *inside* the shelter to stay warm?

He shook his head and paused in scraping the bark off one of the shafts to look across the lake. Too much to know for right now, too much to do. In the trees on the other side of the lake the leaves were changing.

They must have been doing it for a week or more, he thought—why didn't I see it? And now that he noted it he saw that in many other areas the leaves were changing as well; mostly gold, some shades of pink and red, scattered bits of color. And the sky over the lake was different as well. The soft summer clouds were gone and where it was blue it was a flat coppery blue and where the clouds were coming they were a slate gray—and they grew as he watched. Not in thunderheads as in the summer, towering and full of drama, but an almost ugly gray that was all one shade and expanded from the north to cover the sky as if pushed by a large hand. Even as he watched, the patch of blue he had seen at first was gone and all the sky was gray and he could smell rain. Again, not the rain of summer but a cooler, almost cold rain was coming and it made him shiver though it had not started yet.

He went back to his shaving on the arrow shafts, concentrating on the task at hand. Something else he had learned: Do what you can as you can. Trouble, problems, will come no matter what you do, and you must respond as they come.

And indeed, he was having enough trouble with the idea of a war bow. It was all well and good to say he would have a more powerful bow—in the hope that a better weapon would give him more protection—but making one, and the arrows, was harder than he had thought it would be.

It all came down to poking a hole in something to kill it, he thought. That's what weapons were all about, whether it was a gun or a spear or an arrow. Something had to die for him to live and the way to kill it was by poking a hole in it to make it die. He grimaced.

But it was so. The hole had to be poked, the animal killed, and therein lay the difficulty with a war bow. It was one thing to poke a hole in a rabbit or a foolbird. They were small and thin-skinned. It was something else to think of doing it to a large animal.

Once he had shot at a porcupine up in a tree with his light bow, thinking that if he could bring it down and skin it—very carefully—he would get more meat and fat than he did off rabbits and foolbirds. He was amazed to see his arrow bounce harmlessly off the side of the porcupine. If he could not shoot a relatively small animal what could be done to kill or even hurt a larger one?

It was in the strength of the bow, he thought, and the type of arrow. The bow had to be so stiff it would drive the arrow much harder into a larger animal, to get deeper into a vital area, and the arrow had to have some way to cut through and make a larger hole.

The stiffer bow he thought he had already made— though he would have to wait and string it to make certain—but the arrows were a problem. He had stiffer shafts, to take the extra load of a stronger bow, but the points were something else again. He thought on them long and hard all that night while working on the shafts by the fire. He considered the bits of aluminum scrap from the skin of the plane, but they were too thin and soft.

There had been something, a place, some place that could help him and he couldn't make it come to his mind until after he'd gone to bed and was lying looking at the glowing coals of the fire.

Pintner's Sporting Goods Store. It was an old store that he sometimes passed on his way to school, run by an older man named Pintner who had a sign over the door that said he was "Anti-mall." And the store reflected it. There was none of the glitter or modernness of a mall, just some funky shelves and guns and bows and some hockey gear and an old oil stove where unshaven men sat and talked about the old days and spit tobacco juice into old coffee cans.

Brian had not been in the store that many times but on one occasion he'd stopped there to see if Pintner sharpened ice skates and next to the door there'd been a large glass case with a collection of arrowheads arranged in a circle. He had stopped to study them and he had thought then that it was a beautiful collection of intricately carved points, all laid out on red velvet, and he did not then or later think of what they really were: tools for hunting.

Only now, lying in his bag, looking at them in his mind, did it hit him just exactly what they were: arrowheads. Tips for arrows to make them punch holes. Some very small, some large and wide, and all of stone and all with sharp edges.

Those people were the pros, he thought—the Native Americans who had made the points centuries before. They lived all the time as Brian was trying to live now and they had experimented for thousands of years to come up with the designs of the heads. Brian closed his eyes and tried to remember how they had looked.

When he had an image he smoothed a place in the dirt next to the fire and drew five outlines that he thought he remembered correctly and tried to make them roughly the same size as the originals in the collection.

Three were small and he ignored them. Two were quite a bit larger and these he studied in his mind pictures as well as in the lines in the dirt.

There could be only one reason for a larger arrowhead—

to kill a larger animal. They worked that out, he thought. They found after thousands of years that a larger head killed a larger animal. All my research has been done.

Now, he thought, all I have to do is find a way to make stone arrowheads.

He searched his memory, what he had learned in school, seen on television, read in books, and nowhere could he find a picture of anybody saying how stone arrowheads were made.

Well then, start with what you know.

The arrowheads were made of stone. So find a stone that will work, he thought, and went to sleep thinking of all the places around the lake where he had seen stones.

In the morning he awakened famished, as if he hadn't eaten for a week. There were only four fish left in the fish pool and none on the line—which bothered him—and he ate two of the larger fish to take the edge off his hunger.

He would have to hunt today and get meat and set the arrowhead problem aside. In midmorning, after cleaning the camp and trying to hide the pot inside his shelter in case the bear came back, he set off to the north.

In the months that he'd lived on the L-shaped lake and hunted the area, he'd come to know the surrounding region like a large yard. Except for predators, which ranged constantly, looking for food, most animals seemed to stay pretty much in the same location, and because they started there they tended to grow there. North about half a mile it was best for hunting rabbits. There was a large patch—as big as a football field—where an ancient fire had burned the trees off and left brush. Rabbits had hidden there from predators because they could escape into the thick brambles easily. Because they had come there and been able to live there they had increased—as rabbits do—and now there seemed to be rabbits wherever Brian looked in the patch. It was unusual for him to go there without getting several good shots and though he still often missed he had worked out a ratio of five to one: He seemed to get one rabbit for about every five shots on rabbits. The ratio was seven to one on foolbirds.

Although he had hit the last rabbit he shot at, he felt lucky, and he approached the brushy area with an arrow already nocked on the string.

Things never happened as he planned, however, and because he was concentrating on looking for rabbits he very nearly stepped on a foolbird. It blew up under his foot in a flash of leaves and feathers like a grenade detonating and flew off at a quartering angle away and to Brian's left front.

Without thinking he raised the bow, drew and released the arrow and was absolutely flabbergasted to see it fly in a clean line, intersect the flight line of the foolbird and take it neatly through the center of its body.

It cartwheeled to the ground and Brian ran over to it. Though it looked dead, he broke its neck with a quick snap to make certain it was gone.

Incredible, he thought. If I lived to be a hundred and tried it a thousand more times I would never be able to do it again. Just a clean reflexive shot.

But more—he pulled the arrow out of the dead foolbird and wiped the blood off it and turned to walk back to camp with the same arrow on the string. He took five steps and a rabbit jumped out from a bush on his right and in one smooth action he dropped the dead bird, raised the bow, drew the arrow and released it and saw it take the rabbit through the chest at a flat run. It died before he could get to it and he picked it up. That night he cleaned them both and made a stew, boiling them together, and ate the meat and drank the broth until he was packed, full, his stomach rounded and bulging.

Two, he thought—two with the same arrow and both moving and both hit almost perfectly. He took the arrow from the rest of them and propped it in the corner. That, he thought, is my lucky arrow. In the same instant the word *medicine* came into his thought—*It is my medicine arrow*. He had not planned it, not meant to think the phrase, but it came and he knew it was right. It was not a religous idea so much as a way to believe in what he had done, and how he had done it, and from that day on he did not use the arrow again but put it on a small rock ledge. When things were bad he would look to the arrow on the ledge and think of how right it had been: one arrow, two kills, and a full belly all on one day.

That night before he went to sleep, as he lay in his shelter with the light from the fire coming through the opening, he took a stick of charcoal from the fire and drew what he had done on the rock wall above his bed. A stick figure with a bow shooting an arrow at two stick animals, one bird and one rabbit, and lines showing how the same arrow had taken both of them. When he was done he shaded in the animals and the figure of the boy with the charcoal to give them body, working in the flickering light. He wished he had some color to work in as well, to show feathers and fur and blood.

It was not until later, as he lay back just before full-belly contented sleep, that he remembered having seen some pictures in a magazine of the cave paintings in France. Old, he thought, they were the oldest art ever found, according to the article. Painted by ancient, by early man.

Brian burrowed down into the bag and closed his eyes, and the last thing he thought was to wonder if the ancient men who drew in the caves in France ever took two animals with the same arrow . . .

Chapter

FOUR

It was all much harder than he had thought it was going to be—which, of course, might be said for Brian's whole life since the plane crash. But in this case he had somewhere to start. He had made the lighter bow and had tried to make slightly heavier bows, and he thought that making a really powerful weapon would be simply like doubling the smaller ones.

It was more than double. Because everything was stronger, there were difficulties that would not have occurred to him.

Rain came on the third day of drying the heavy bows. Luckily, Brian thought, they had dried enough, and set them inside the shelter until the rain stopped.

Except that it didn't stop. In the summer when it rained it might last half a day or even a full day, but then it cleared off and dried out. Even violent storms, like the tornado that had caught him and brought the plane up, were short-lived.

But this was fall, and fall rains were a whole new dimension in weather. It started to rain from a low, gray sky and it didn't rain hard and it didn't rain soft. It just . . . kept . . . raining. Brian almost went crazy with it. By the end of the first whole day it was all he could do to find dry wood to keep the fire going. By the end of the second day of constant drizzle he found himself looking at the sky hoping to see a hole, anything with bright light.

But it rained steadily for five days and while it rained it turned colder, so that by the fifth day Brian felt as if he were freezing. The only way he could find dry wood was by looking for dead logs that had hung up off the ground, and then by breaking limbs off beneath them where they weren't quite as soaked as they were on top. By the time he got enough wood to burn for a few hours and keep the fire going against the rain he was so soaked that it took all the time the wood burned just to get him warm and dry enough to go out again to search for more wood.

The inside of his sleeping bag was damp at first, then flat wet, and finally as soaked from his body and the humidity as if it had been out in the open rain.

But still worse, with the rain he did not think he could hunt and so had no food. On the fourth day he found a four-pound northern pike on his fishline and he ate it at one sitting, saving the guts and head for bait.

But he got no more fish and by the sixth day, when it was clear that it wasn't going to stop raining—he believed now that it would *never* stop raining—by the end of the sixth day he decided that he would simply have to live in cold rain for the rest of his life, and the morning of the seventh day he sat in his bag, looked outside and said:

"To hell with it. I'm going hunting."

And he did. He strung his bow and took his arrows—

after touching his medicine arrow for luck—and in a tattered T-shirt with the hunting knife at his belt he set off into the rain.

Hunting took his mind off the cold and he found to his immense surprise that hunting was better during a rain than it was in clear weather. Game could hole up for a day or two of bad weather but animals were governed by the same physics as Brian, and rain or no rain, cold or no cold, they had to come out and eat.

He took a foolbird not forty feet from the camp and got four shots at two different rabbits within another twenty yards. He missed the rabbits but was satisfied with the foolbird and went back to build up the sputtering fire one more time and made a hot stew—including the heart and liver and a tough muscle he thought must be the gizzard, which he had come to like—and ate it all before falling sound asleep in his wet bag.

He slept hard, in spite of being cold and damp, but in the middle of the night he opened his eyes, instantly awake, and waited for his eyes and mind to tell him what had awakened him.

No noise, nothing, and then he realized that it had stopped. There was no rain falling and he peeked out of the shelter to see a night sky filled with stars and a sliver of a moon and he looked up at them and said softly, "Thank you," and went back to sleep.

In the morning it was cold, truly cold. He saw his breath in the dawn sunlight coming through the opening and when he looked outside he saw a ring of ice four or five feet out from the edge of the lake all around the shore.

He stood up out of the bag, shivering, and got the fire going until it blazed merrily and then sat close to it, watching the sun come up while he warmed himself. When he had stopped shivering he brought his sleeping bag outside and spread it in the sunlight away from the fire so that no sparks would hit it and left it there to dry.

Within an hour the temperature was in the comfort range and Brian stretched and let the sun cook his bones for a few minutes. The ground was still damp but he sat on a dry rock and looked at the blue sky and felt the hot sun and it was as if the days and days of rain had never happened. A kind of lethargy came over him and he just wanted to sit in the sun and try to forget the last week. He closed his eyes and dozed for a few minutes but a new sound, high and almost cackling, cut into his doze and he opened his eyes to see a flock of geese high above heading south, migrating.

It was a reminder—it did not get things done, sitting— and in the back of his mind was the thought that what he had just had was a warning. A week of cold rain to show him how poor he was, how completely unready he was for what he knew now was coming. And today the geese to cap it.

He must work now, work hard or he would not make it. No matter how nice the weather might be he knew he had no time left.

First the shelter. He had to make the shelter coldproof and rainproof. That meant sealing the fire inside and closing the door in some way, but he thought the smoke would drive him out.

Still, he thought, they did it. The people who came before him had tents and tipis and caves and they did not have stoves. So how did they do it?

He took kindling into the shelter and made a small fire, and closed off the opening to see what would happen. As he had predicted, the smoke quickly filled the small enclosure and drove him coughing and spitting out into the air.

He had to let the smoke out. They must have known a way—what did they do? Tipis just let it come out the top through a hole. He'd seen that in movies, old Westerns on television.

Brian went to where his wall met the rock and made a hole about a foot across just above where he had made the fire, then tried it all again.

This time when he closed the door and put some sticks on the fire it started to smoke again but as the heat developed it rose and carried a small draft through the hole in the ceiling. There was a moment of smoke; then it all magically cleared and Brian was sitting in a snug little hut with a fire warming his face. Clearly it would take only a small blaze to keep the little shelter warm, which meant less wood would be required.

The side of the shelter was still far from airtight but about this Brian knew exactly what to do. He had spent one whole day watching a family of beaver mix mud and sticks to make a watertight dam. He spent three hours bringing up double armfuls of fresh mud from the lake to pack into the low wall with sticks and leaves. When he was done he covered it with another layer of brush to protect the mud and when it dried by nightfall he had a truly weathertight shelter. He still had to seal the door but that night he sat with a fire warming the inside of his home and knew that as long as he had wood—and he was living in the middle of a forest—he would stay warm no matter what kind of weather came. He slept so soundly that the bear could have come in again and torn the place apart and he would not have known it.

In the morning he mudded the door and set it aside to dry and used more mud to make a seal on the wall, smooth and tight. Then he set back to work on the arrowhead problem.

He went to the lakeshore and looked for stones that would make an arrowhead. There were rocks everywhere and he must have looked at a hundred, turning them this way and that, tapping them against each other. None of them worked or fit or seemed right and he stopped and thought again about the arrowhead collection.

They weren't just stones in the shape of arrowheads. They had been worked, chiseled someway from larger stones to get the shape and edge. But what kind of stone and how? Wasn't it some special type of rock, something that would flake off in sharp edges?

He had his hatchet on his belt and went back to the shore and started hitting rocks with the flat side of the hatchet. They just shattered and didn't make any kind of sharp point. One rock chipped off a flake about three inches long and in the right shape but when he picked up the flake and tapped it with the back of the hatchet it fell into a dozen unusable pieces.

Flint. There, the word came to him. They weren't just arrowheads, they were *flint* arrowheads—maybe they had to be flint to chip right.

So all he had to do was find some flint.

He went back to the lakeshore and looked at the rock supply again, smashing rocks with the back of the hatchet to see if any of them were made of flint. In truth, he didn't really know what to look for, except that he remembered that flint and steel would spark when they hit.

He had smashed four or five more rocks looking for sparks when it came to him. There was a rock embedded in the wall of his shelter. He had thrown his hatchet at the porcupine the night he got stuck in the leg and the hatchet had showered sparks and led him to make fire.

It was there, in the fire rock. He had forgotten the rock because there had been matches and lighters in the survival pack he'd retrieved from the plane, and he hadn't had to use the rock again.

He went and looked at it for the first time in more than a month, studied it. It was a dark rock; it had depth and seemed to have fracture lines or flaws in it. He struck it with the hatchet and smiled when he saw sparks, remembering the night the porcupine had come. But the rock didn't shatter or flake. He looked at it from a different angle and saw a small ridge, little more than a line, and this time he aimed carefully and struck the line with the blunt corner of the hatchet, using a sharp tap with a little more muscle.

This time it cracked and a flake as wide as two fingers and three inches long fell to the ground beneath the rock.

He picked it up.

"Ouch!" He dropped it. The edge was as sharp as a razor and it cut his finger slightly. He sucked the blood away and picked the flake up more carefully, and turned it to the light. It had a slightly oval shape, pointed on one end and rounded on the other. Both sides leading down to the point were so sharp they would shave hair off the back of his arm.

All it needed to make it a true arrowhead was a pair of notches, one on either side of the rounded end. He put the flake on a flat rock and held it in place with his foot, vising it down tightly, while he chipped away at the notch positions with the tip of his hunting knife. He started with too big a piece and it broke the whole tip of the oval off and left the flake with a flat rear end. From then on he took tiny chips, each no bigger than the head of a pin, until he had an arrowhead that resembled those in the collection. It was not finished as well as the ancients had finished theirs, but it was sharp and tapered the right way and had a notch for tying it onto the shaft.

He took one of the shafts for the war bow arrows and

split the grain on the end with the knife. He worked the point back into the split so that the notch was slightly recessed into the wood.

He had nothing with which to tie it into position and was casting around for a piece of string—nonexistent except for the original bowstring from his first bow or he would have used it long ago—when he saw the tree with the rabbit skins.

Whenever he took a rabbit he skinned it carefully and stretched the skin on the sides of an oak, holding it with wooden pegs driven into the bark until it was dry. He had not found a use for the skins yet but he hated to waste anything and thought something might come along. When they dried they were like thick paper with hair on one side, dry and crinkly and easy to tear. But the last hide he'd put up during the rain had not dried yet and he took it off the tree. Still damp, the hide had a strength to it and might make a kind of cord. He used the knife to cut strips from the rabbit skin and used one of the rawhide strips to tightly wrap and tie the point onto the split shaft.

When he was finished it seemed to be tight enough, and he had heard that rawhide shrinks when it dries, so that might make it even better. Of course the hair was still on the skin and stuck out all around and made the arrow look like a pom-pom, but a quick pass over the flames in the fire pit burned all the hair off, and when he was done he trimmed the ends of the lacing and it looked good.

"Almost professional." He set the shaft aside and went

back to the fire rock—he was already thinking of it as the arrow stone—and scrutinized it once more. Where he had broken the flake off it left two more edges, lines that looked the same as the first one, and he used the back of the hatchet to strike them the way he'd hit the first one.

Two more flakes came off, almost identical to the first one, and left two more lines. When he tapped those it happened again, and again until he had nine flake-points. He took them back to his work rock and clamped them with his foot and worked tie-notches into the shanks with the point of his knife and fitted them to the shafts with green rabbit hide and all of this, rock to points, in one day.

Just as bad things could snowball, Brian found that good things could come fast as well. While he was working with the rabbit skin in the cool evening he turned it to get a better angle and the hair brushed his hand and felt warm and he realized he'd found a way to stay warm.

He had fifteen dried skins and he brought them into the shelter at dark. He had not eaten again but the hunger was not as bad now because he was excited. Working in the firelight, he trimmed the hides to make them clean-edged and rectangular. He used one hide for lacing, cutting thin strips off the edge with his knife—the first-aid scissors were too small to help—and started lacing the others together to form a large rectangle. It took some time because he had no needle and used the point of the knife to punch a small hole through the sides of the hides and then a sharp-

41

ened twig to push the lacing through. Also the laces weren't long and he could only "sew" seven or eight inches before he had to tie it off and use a new lace and by the time he had four hides sewn together he could feel exhaustion taking him down. He crawled into his bag and slept hard and didn't awaken until well after dawn.

Hunger awakened with him and he knew he had to hunt before he worked more on the hides so he took the light bow and arrows and went to the foolbird area. This time luck wasn't with him and he missed three birds before he got a shot at a rabbit that hit. He cleaned it and used the green hide for lacing and started sewing again while his stew cooked and before he knew it he was back in the shelter again, working in the light from the fire, his stomach full and his fingers flying. But this time before he fell asleep he had finished sewing the rabbit skins into a rectangle roughly two feet wide by nearly six feet long.

"It would make a good rug," he said, crawling into the bag to sleep at what he thought must be three or four in the morning.

Just before sleep came he heard the wolves. It sounded like two of them, high, keening howls as they sang to each other and then a crash in the brush as they chased something—maybe a deer. He had not heard from them in almost two weeks. There had been a time when the howls would have frightened him, given him an eerie feeling, but now he smiled. They must have gotten caught in the weather if it had taken them so long to run a circuit of their range, and he supposed they would mark the edge of their territory on the way through. He would have to go up and re-mark his own—the rains would have taken the smell away—the first thing in the morning.

Good hunting, he thought at the wolves—have a good hunt. A good hunt was everything.

FIVE

The morning dawned cold—more ice around the edge of the lake and the geese and ducks were flying almost constantly now—and after he rekindled the fire Brian went to work at once on the rabbit skins. He folded the rectangle over on itself with the fur on the inside and sewed up the sides, leaving two holes about six inches across at the top on each side, then cut a hole large enough for his head in the fold and pulled the whole thing down over his head, sticking his arms through the holes as he did so.

It made a perfect vest. Well, he thought, looking down at himself—maybe not perfect. It actually looked pretty tacky, with bits of dried flesh still stuck to the hides here and there and the crude lacing. But it was warm, very warm, and within moments he was sweating and realized that it was more than he needed and had to take it off.

He set it aside and was about to get back to work on the arrows—he still had to fletch them, put feathers on the shafts—when he remembered the wolves. He trotted up to mark his boundary stump and came around a corner near the stump and stopped dead.

Facing him was a wolf, a big male, his head covered with fresh blood. He was holding a large piece of meat with a bone in the center in his mouth and he didn't growl or look at Brian with anything but mild curiosity. They stood that way, Brian with no weapon and nothing in his mind but peeing on a stump, and the wolf holding the meat, and then the wolf turned and trotted off to the left and was gone.

But he had come from the right, Brian thought—somewhere to the right—and as he watched, another wolf came by from the right with another piece of meat, though slightly smaller, and trotted easily off to the left, following the first one.

And Brian was alone. He stood, waiting, and when no more wolves came he relaxed his shoulders, which had been straining, and thought of what he had just seen.

They must have been the wolves that had sung the night before just as he went to sleep. They had hunted well and he smiled, thinking how they must feel—how he felt when it went well—and turned to go to his stump, when he thought again.

They had been carrying meat. Fresh meat. He did not know what kind it was but it must have been a large animal. Maybe a deer. And they seemed to be done with it.

Maybe there's something left of the kill, he thought; if I can find it maybe there's something left I can use. He started off the way the wolves had come but stopped again, thought a moment, then trotted back to camp and got his knife and hatchet and fire-hardened spear. Knowing the woods as he did, he knew there was a chance that he would not be the only thing looking at the wolves' kill.

He started back up in the direction the wolves had come from, and hadn't gone a hundred yards when he came to it.

It had been a deer, a young doe. There were dozens around and Brian had thought of hunting them, but his weapons were light and it was hard to get close to them. So he'd settled for rabbits and fish and foolbirds.

She had been the crash he had heard in the night when the wolves had howled, and he stopped before the kill to read sign. The doe was on the near side of a small clearing. She must have run out of the far side with the wolves nearly on her and they had caught her and held her while they tore at her to kill her.

She must have thrashed around a good deal because the grass was bloody across thirty or so feet and the ground was torn up. But they'd taken her down. Brian could see her tracks where they'd come into the clearing, and where the dirt was torn he could see the wolf tracks and he closed his eyes for a moment and imagined what it had been like—the deer running through the brush, the wolves gaining, then setting their teeth in her and dragging her back and down . . .

He shook his head and came back to reality. Most of her was gone. They had started at the rear, pulling and eating, and had taken both back legs off and up into the guts, as well as chewing at the neck. All that was really left was the head and neck and front shoulders and tattered bits of hide, the whole thing looking like a roadkill hit by a semi.

Brian smiled. It's a treasure, he thought, and actually

started to salivate and then smiled more widely as he had a fleeting image of back in the world and what they would think if they could see him now, salivating over what amounted to a roadkill.

He would have to work fast. Other predators—a bear, foxes, perhaps more wolves—could come along at any moment and until he got to the protection of the fire he wasn't sure he could hold his new wealth.

The portion of the doe that was left weighed less than fifty pounds and he dragged it easily at first but then, seeing that it left a blood mark as it skidded along, and worried that it would be too easy to follow, he picked up the carcass and threw it over his shoulder and carried it.

At the shelter he put it down and put more wood on the fire and took out his knife. First it would have to be skinned. The skin toward the rear was torn and shredded where the wolves had ripped and fed but it was largely whole on her chest and neck and he worked carefully. First a cut down from the underside of her chin to the middle of her chest, and here was his first surprise. Rabbits were easy to skin—the hide almost fell off them. The doe's skin was stuck tight to the meat and did not come off with simply pulling at it, the way a rabbit skin did. Brian had to use the tip of the knife to cut the skin away from the flesh, peeling it back a quarter of an inch at a time, and it took him the better part of an hour, working constantly, to get the hide loose, cutting it off the front legs and up the neck to the back of the head.

The doe's eyes bothered him at first. They were large

and brown and open and seemed to be watching him as he turned and cut and pulled, and he apologized for what had happened to her, what he was doing to her.

It did not ease his discomfort but he hoped the spirit of the deer knew what he was feeling and he promised that none of what was there would be wasted.

And what a lot of it there was—more than he'd seen since he crashed. The hide—much tougher and thicker than the rabbit skins—was big enough to nearly make another vest and he laid it near the side of his shelter to dry while he worked at the meat.

The wolves had fed until they were gorged and must have then taken what they could carry back to their den, but he was amazed at how much meat there was left. He started cutting it off in strips, lean red meat, which he laid on a flat rock. Just off one shoulder there was more meat than he'd ever seen together in one place outside a supermarket. A good six or seven pounds, with no bone in it, and then the other shoulder and then on top going up the neck and when he was finally done—just at dark—he figured he had twenty-five or thirty pounds of meat.

He made a huge stew, boiling close to six pounds of meat sitting by the fire in his rabbit-skin vest as the evening chill came down. Then he ate, and ate and ate, and when he was done there was still meat and broth left. He dozed, slept and awakened in the middle of the night and ate some more, drank some more of the broth, and there was *still* some left.

He awakened in the morning with a stomach still bulging full and grease on his lips and something close to joy in his heart.

He was not done with the body of the doe. The head bothered him—the way her eyes seemed to see things—and he separated it from the neck bones and took it up and set it in the fork of a tree well off the ground and looking out over the lake. He wasn't sure why but it seemed the right thing to do and he thanked her again for her meat before turning back to work.

The freezes at night had done away with the flies so they didn't bother the meat and he spread the pieces out to give them air and by the middle of the afternoon he could see they were drying into a kind of jerky in the sun. But before that he went to work on the bones. There was still a lot of meat on them and he chopped them up with the hatchet and kept a pot boiling all day to boil the meat and marrow from them. When it was finally done—again, in late afternoon—he was surprised to see the liquid in the pot become semihard, like Jell-O, and turn into a thick mass full of bits of cooked meat.

This he ate for the evening meal—or about half of it—spooning it in thick glops, and when he was at last back in his shelter, the meat stored safely in the rear and the pot set aside from the fire for the night (still half full) he felt like the richest man on the earth.

It was very hard to concentrate on working. Everything in him wanted to sleep now—he'd never been so full and the shelter was warm and snug and all he really wanted to do was close his eyes and sleep and end the day.

But he could not forget the bear attack, or the rain and cold, and he knew that the good weather and his luck wouldn't last and he had really no time to waste.

He took the arrows out and rummaged around in the survival pack for his feather stash. He had found early on that foolbird feathers from the wing and tail worked the best for arrows and he had saved every wing and tail feather from every foolbird that he had shot and he took them out now.

These arrows were different. They were heavier and he worried that the width of the point would catch the air and counteract the feathers in some way. The solution, he felt, was to make the feathers longer.

He selected only two feathers for each arrow but left them a full six inches long and shaved a flat side with the knife the full length of each feather so that it would fit the arrow shaft.

He attached the arrows with pieces of thread from his old windbreaker, wrapping them at the front and the rear and then smearing them with bits of warmed pine sap—a trick he had learned when he had leaned against some sap on a tree and stuck to it—to protect the thread.

He did three arrows, working slowly and carefully before going at last to sleep. Once again he slept so hard that he awakened with his head jammed into the ground and his neck stiff from not moving all night.

Because of all the meat from the doe he did not have to hunt for days now, at least ten or twelve, maybe two weeks, and he worked all day on the arrows and bow, sitting next to the shelter in the warm sun, snacking on the jellied meat now and then.

By dark this day all nine arrows were finished. He had used the hunting knife as a scraper to shape the limbs of the bow more equally and to put in notches for the string to get it ready to string the next day for the first shooting trials. He was just leaning back, half cocky about how well things were going, when he smelled the skunk.

He had run into skunks before, of course, saw them all the time, but had only had the one really bad experience when he got sprayed directly. He knew they moved at night, hunting, and didn't seem very afraid of anything. He looked out of the shelter opening carefully.

The skunk wasn't four feet away, looking in at him at the shelter and the fire and as he watched, it whipped up its rear end and tipped its tail over and aimed directly at his face.

I'm dead, he thought, and froze. For a long time they stayed that way, Brian holding his breath waiting to be nailed, and the skunk aiming at him. But the skunk didn't spray, just aimed and held it.

He's hungry, Brian thought. That's all. He's hunting and he's hungry. Slowly Brian reached to his right, where the meat was stored back in the corner, and took a piece of the venison. With a smooth, slow movement he tossed the meat out to the right of the skunk. For a split second he thought it was over. The skunk's tail jerked when the meat hit the ground but then its nose twitched as it smelled it and it lowered its tail, turned and started eating the meat.

Brian carefully reached out to the side and pulled the door back over the opening and left the skunk outside eating.

Great, he thought, crawling back into his bag to sleep— I've got a pet skunk who's a terrorist. If I quit feeding him he'll spray me. Just great. His eyes closed and he sighed. Maybe he'll be gone in the morning.

Chapter

SIX

In the morning he pushed the door to the side gingerly, looking both ways. He didn't see the skunk and he pushed the door all the way open and went outside. Still no skunk. Before heading back for the trench he had dug for a toilet he pulled the door back over the opening—no sense taking chances—and then trotted off into the woods.

When he came back he looked all around the area and still couldn't see the skunk and he shrugged. It must have moved on.

He kindled an outside fire using coals from the shelter fire and soon had a small cooking fire going. The cold lasted longer now into the morning and the ice had moved farther out into the lake, almost forty feet from the shore all around. The rabbit-skin vest and the fire felt especially good.

He took the last of the jellied meat in the pot, added a piece of red venison, and put it on the side of the fire to cook while he took stock of his situation. The shelter was done, or as done as he could get it, and almost airtight and warm when he had a fire going inside. He had nine arrows finished, which seemed like a lot. How many times would he have to defend himself? Besides, even if he used all the arrows he could get more tips from the arrow stone, and the wood shafts would be there in the winter as well.

Winter.

The word stopped him. He knew nothing about it. At home in upstate New York, there was snow, sometimes a lot of it, and cold at times, cold enough to make his ears sting, but he could get inside, and he had good warm clothes. Here, he suspected, the winter would be a lot worse, but he didn't know how much worse or how to prepare for it.

Just then the meat was done and at exactly that moment, as he pulled the pot off the fire, the skunk came waddling around the end of the rock, stopped four feet away and raised its tail.

"What . . ." Brian winced, waiting, but the skunk did not spray and Brian took a piece of meat from the pot and threw it on the ground next to it. The skunk lowered its tail, smelled the meat, and when it proved too hot to eat, it backed away and raised its tail again.

"Listen, you little robber—I'm sorry it's too hot. You'll just have to wait until it cools . . ."

The skunk kept its tail up, but lowered it a bit and seemed to understand, and in a moment when the meat cooled it picked up the chunk and disappeared with it around the corner of the large rock that was the back wall of Brian's shelter.

"Where are you going?"

Brian stood up and followed at a distance, moving

slowly, and when he came around the rock the skunk was gone, disappeared completely.

"But . . ."

Brian walked all around the end, back again, and was on his second loop when he saw some grass wiggling at the edge where the rock met the ground. The grass here was thick and about a foot tall and hid the dirt from view. Brian moved closer and saw some fresh earth and a hole beneath the rock and as he watched he saw black-and-white fur moving down inside the hole.

"You're living here?" Brian shook his head. "You've moved *in* on me?"

The skunk stopped moving inside for a moment, then started again, and while Brian watched, little spurts of dirt came out of the entrance as the skunk dug back in under the rock.

Brian turned away. "Wonderful—I've got a roommate with a terminal hygiene problem . . ."

Inside of four days a routine was established. The skunk came to the entrance in the morning, flicked its tail in the air and waited to be fed. Brian fed it and it went back to its burrow until the next morning.

It wasn't exactly friendship, but soon Brian smiled when he saw the skunk. He named it Betty after deciding that it was a female and that it looked like his aunt, who was low and round and waddled the same way. He looked forward to seeing it.

After developing the acquaintance with the skunk Brian

had gone back to work on the heavy bow. The arrows were done but he had yet to string the bow and was stymied on where to get a string long enough until he saw the cord at the end of the sleeping bag. It was braided nylon, one eighth of an inch thick and close to six feet long—enough to go around the bag twice when it was rolled up.

The cord was sewn into the end of the bag but he sharpened the knife on his sharpening rock and used the point to open the stitching enough to free the cord.

It proved to be difficult to string the bow. In spite of his scraping and shaping, the limbs were still very stout and the bow bent only with heavy pressure. He tied the string to one end, then put the tied end in a depression in a rock on the ground and used his weight to pull down the top end while he tied the cord in place.

It hummed when he plucked it and the strength of the wood seemed to sing in the cord. He took four of the arrows and moved to a dirt hummock near the lakeshore.

He put an arrow in the bow and fitted it to the string, raised the bow and looked down the shaft at the target and drew the arrow back.

Or tried to. When it was halfway to his chin the bow seemed to double in strength and he was shaking with the exertion by the time he got the feathers all the way back and the cord seemed to be cutting through his fingers. He released quickly, before he had time to aim properly, and saw the arrow crease the top of the hummock, skip onto the lake ice, jump off the ice and fly across the open water in the middle and land skittering across the ice on the far side of the lake—a good two hundred yards.

At the same time the string slapped his arm so hard it seemed to tear the skin off and the rough front end of the feathers cut the top of his hand as they passed over it.

"Wow . . ."

He could not see the arrow but he knew where it had gone and would walk around the lake later and retrieve it. Now he had to practice. He changed the angle he was shooting at so that the arrows wouldn't go across the lake if he missed—*when* he missed, he thought, smiling—and moved closer to the hummock.

It was hard to judge the strength of the pull of the bow. He guessed fifty, sixty pounds of pull were required to get the string back to his chin, and every shot hurt his arm and fingers and hand. But it was worth it. The arrows left the bow so fast that he couldn't see them fly and they hit so hard that two of them drove on through the hummock and kept going for fifteen or twenty yards and broke the stone tips.

He made new tips that night and it was while he was making them that he knew he would be hunting bigger game. It was strange how the thought came, or how it just seemed to be there. He had made the bow for protection, had thought only in terms of protection all the while he was making arrows, but somewhere along the way the knowledge that he would use it to hunt was just there.

Maybe it was eating the meat from the doe that had

done it. There was so much of it, and it tasted so good and was easier to deal with than the smaller animals. Whatever the reason, when he aimed at the hummock to practice he saw the chest of a deer.

He shot all that day, until his shoulders were sore and he had broken an arrow and two more tips by hitting small rocks along the ground. Then at dark he built a fire, cooked some meat, fed Betty, who arrived just as the meat was done, and retired to the shelter to fix arrows.

He would hunt big tomorrow, he thought. He would try to get a deer.

Chapter

SEVEN

He didn't know the time but somewhere in the middle of the night he awakened suddenly. He had come to rely on his senses and he knew something had changed to snap him awake that way and he lay with his eyes wide in the dark, listening, smelling, trying to see.

He did not have long to wait.

There was a soft rustle, then a whoofing sound and the whole wall of the shelter peeled away from the rock as if caught in an earthquake, away and down and Brian—still in his bag—was looking up in the dark at the enormous form of a bear leaning over him.

There was no time to react, to move, to do anything.

Meat, Brian had time to think—he's smelled the venison and come for it. He's come for the mea—

And it was true. The bear had come for the meat but the problem was that Brian lay between the bear and the meat, and the bear cuffed him to the side. As it was it wasn't much of a cuff—nowhere near what the bear could have done, which would have broken Brian's legs—but the bag was zipped and Brian became tangled in it and couldn't move fast enough to stay out of the way so the bear hit him again.

This time hard. The blow took Brian in the upper thigh and even through the bag it was solid enough to nearly dislocate his hip.

He cried out. "Ahhhh . . ."

The bear stopped dead in the darkness. Brian could see the head turn to look back and down at him, a slow turning, huge and full of threat, and the bear's breath washed over him and he thought I am going to die now. All this that I have done and I'm going to die because a bear wants to eat and I am in the way. He could see the bear's teeth as it showed them and he couldn't, simply couldn't do anything; couldn't move, couldn't react. It was over.

The bear started to move down toward Brian and then hesitated, stopped and raised its head again and turned to look back over its shoulder to the left.

Half a beat and Brian lay still, staring up at the bear. But now a new smell, over the smell of the bear; a rank, foul, sulfurous and gagging smell as the bear turned and took a full shot of skunk spray directly in the eyes.

Betty had arrived. Whether she'd just been out hunting and had come back or had been awakened and surprised or simply didn't like bears very much—whatever the reason she had dumped a full load in the bear's face.

The effect was immediate and devastating.

"Rowwrrrmph!"

The bear seemed to turn inside itself, knocking Brian farther to the side, and rolled backward out of the shelter area, slamming its head back and forth on the ground, trying to clear its eyes, hacking and throwing up as it vanished in the night.

Brian looked to the source of all this. Betty stood near the end of the shelter, still with her tail raised, only now aimed at Brian. She twitched it once, then again, and Brian shook his head.

"I'm sorry. I just didn't think you'd be thinking of food . . ." He took a piece of meat from the pile—a big one—and tossed it to her and she lowered her tail, picked up the meat and waddled off into the dark in the direction of her burrow.

Brian lay back in his bag. His shelter was a mess, the wall tipped over, and his hip hurt, but it wasn't raining and the bag was warm. He could fix things up in the morning.

The stink of skunk was everywhere—much of what Betty had shot at the bear had gone around it and hit the wall— but Brian didn't mind. In fact, he thought, I've grown kind of fond of it. I'll have to make sure to give her extra food. It was like having a pet nuclear device.

He went to sleep smiling.

In the morning he found that the damage was not as extreme as he'd thought. The bear had tipped the wall away and down but the dried mud had held it together and Brian—after four heaving tries—tipped it back up and against the rock. He chopped a hole in the thin ice near the edge of the lake and brought up new mud to pack in around the seam and inside an hour it was as good as new.

Then he reviewed his thinking. The war bow wouldn't help—at least not as a protective device. He'd shot it and made it work for him but in the dark, in the night in the shelter, there was no way he could have gotten the bow aligned or an arrow into the bear. And god knew what would have happened if he *had* hit the bear with an arrow—especially if he'd missed anything vital. The bear would have been really mad then—even Betty wouldn't have been able to stop the thing.

Perhaps, he thought, a lance—a killing lance. If he used the same principle as with the arrows . . .

He went back to the stone he'd been chipping arrowheads from and studied it. He would need a wider, longer head, and the flakes came off too small for a spear. Near it there were other black stones, however, and he tapped at them with the back of the hatchet, knocking off flakes until he hit one that had a bigger pattern. Three times he hit, and took off flakes that were irregular or that broke in the middle. But on the fourth try he came away with a piece almost as wide as his palm and about seven inches long, tapering to a sharp point and with two edges like razors.

He worked tie-notches into the round end and mounted the point in one of his hardwood spears, carefully splitting the wood back and then tying the head in place with a thin strip of deer hide—which proved to be much tougher than the rabbit skin—and burning the hair off when he was done.

He hefted the lance and held it out, bracing with his arm. It wouldn't do any good to throw, but for in close, like last night—if he had to use it—the head should cause some damage. Or at least discourage a bear. He nodded. Good. If nothing else, it gave him a feeling of security.

Later he would think on how strange things were. He would never see the bear again and inside the shelter he would never be threatened again.

Yet the lance would save his life.

Part Two

WINTER

Chapter

EIGHT

He awakened when he had slept enough, and looked out of the shelter by cracking the door. It was cold and low and gray and raining, a dismal rain much like the one that had lasted so long earlier in the fall, and he kindled the fire with dry wood he'd set aside the night before when he'd seen the clouds moving in. Soon the inside of the shelter was cheery and warm, the smoke working its way out of the hole at the top, and he wished he'd thought to bring water in the night before and also wished he didn't have to do what he had to do now.

But he couldn't fight it and at last he pulled himself out of the bag, grabbed the hatchet and the largest aluminum pot and plunged out into the rain. As fast as possible, standing barefoot on the freezing, wet ground, he went to the bathroom and then ran to the lake and chopped his watering hole open—it had frozen thinly overnight—and filled the pan and ran back to the shelter.

He slid the door back in place and put the pot on the fire and dropped a piece of venison into it to make a breakfast stew.

The meat was getting low. He had stretched the wolf-killed doe as far as he could, trying to ration it and eat smaller amounts, but he'd have to hunt within four or five days.

He put a piece of meat outside the door for Betty, surprised that she wasn't there already, and leaned back to think.

In the past few days it had become colder. The weather had a kind of steady feel to it, as if it was not going to get warmer but would stay cold, and he had to face some truths.

He simply wasn't ready for cold weather. Oh, he thought, the shelter was all right. And the woods were full of fuel.

But his clothing was pitiful. His jeans were holding together—just—but his tennis shoes were about gone, his socks long since used to shreds, and on top all he had was a T-shirt (also nearly in pieces) and the rabbit-skin vest.

I am, he thought, a mess. He was tempted to smile except that it wasn't really funny. He could sit in the shelter and stay warm but unless he could hunt he would die and he couldn't hunt unless he had something to wear to keep from freezing.

To death, he thought, the truth sliding in like a snake. I could freeze to death. Not quite yet—it wasn't that cold yet—but soon. He didn't know northern winters but he knew it would get cold enough to kill him and freeze him solid.

He took stock again. No clothing, although he still had some rabbit hides, which he could sew into sleeves for his vest. There was also the hide from the doe. He looked at it and thought that he might get a pair of moccasins out of it. They would be crude but if he stitched them with the hair on the inside and made them big enough to wear over his tattered tennis shoes they would help.

He set to work on what he could do and spent all of that day sewing the rest of the rabbit skins into two tubes, which he attached as sleeves to the vest. When he tried it on everything crackled, as if he were wearing paper, but it seemed to hold together and he slept that night feeling slightly better about his future.

The next morning he checked the weather—still raining, and colder than it had been the previous morning—and then set to work making footgear.

It proved both easier and harder than he had thought it would be. The easy part was making a pattern. He just stood on the dry skin and marked around his foot with a piece of charcoal from the fire pit. When he'd cut out the two bottoms he cut two rectangles from the remaining hide and stitched—with some effort as the hide was thick and tough—the two pieces into rough cylinders. Then he sewed each of the tubes down to the sole, attaching it all around the edge, and when he was done he had two clunky boots that he could stick his tennis shoes down into; with the hair on the inside they felt warm the minute he stuck his feet into them. He used the last bits of hide to cut two strips to use for lacing to pull the tops of the cylinders tight to his legs—they hit about midcalf—and it was here he learned how to soften leather.

The deer hide was dried and working with it was about

like working with thin wood. It had no give and was brittle and hard and very, very tough. It was all he could do to sew the cylinders to the bottom using thin-cut hide for lacing and punching holes with the tip of the knife. But the two straps that went around the top had to be soft enough to tie off. He thought of using the fishing line for thread but didn't want to waste it. Then he found that by working the leather—first between his fingers and then by pulling it over a piece of wood that stuck out of the wall—he could soften it. It never got truly soft and supple like tanned deer hide, but it was workable and got the job done.

He gathered more wood just before dark and went to sleep that night dreaming of punching holes in leather with the tip of the knife—the image burned into his mind from sitting all day sewing.

Sometime that night, near the middle, it grew quiet and the change awakened him. He listened for a time and realized that the rain had stopped and he snuggled back in the bag thinking that with no rain the next day he would hunt.

In the morning he awakened and knew instantly that something had changed. Something about the sound. No. The lack of it. There was no sound. Normally he could hear birds in the morning, or the wind rustling.

Now there was nothing.

He crawled out of the bed and opened the door of the shelter. Or tried to. It seemed to be stuck, frozen in place. He pushed harder and finally half stood, crouched, and pushed out with his shoulder against the door.

At first it still didn't move and only when he crouched

back and slammed into it with his shoulder did the door fall away, letting him look outside.

It nearly blinded him.

The entire world was white, bright white with new morning sun glaring off and through it and so intense that it made his temples hurt.

Snow had fallen in the night. Soft, large flakes, nearly four inches deep everywhere. On limbs, logs, the ground, on the lake ice—all over, an even four inches.

And it was cold. Colder than it had been so far. His nostril hairs seemed to stick together when he breathed and the air caught in his throat. The world was so incredibly, wonderfully, stunningly beautiful that for a full minute all he could do was stare.

"Ohh . . ."

He had seen pictures of the woods with snow and had seen snow in the park and in the city but this was different. He was *in* it, inside the snowy scene, and the beauty of it became part of him.

He stepped outside the shelter and as he stepped into the snow realized that he was barefoot. He jumped back inside and put on his tennis shoes and fur boots and the rabbit-skin shirt and moved back outside.

He had never seen anything so clean. Because it was all new there wasn't a mark, not a track in the surface of the snow, and he took four or five paces just to look back at his tracks.

"It's like a bigfoot," he said aloud. And indeed, the boots left a large, rounded hole for a footprint.

He moved around, did his toilet—drawing a picture in the snow when he did—and was amazed how well the boots worked, kept his feet warm and comfortable. As he came close to the shelter he saw a mouse appear almost magically out of the snow, run across the surface for three feet and then dive under again.

Brian moved to where the mouse had run and studied its tracks. Little dots in a parallel line with a small line in the middle where the tail dragged.

But clean, he thought, and neat and so easy to see and follow and everything, everything that moved in the woods would leave tracks.

Would be easy to see.

Would be easy to follow.

Would be much easier to hunt.

He still had some venison left but he decided to hunt. Because the snow was new and he'd never hunted in snow, because the sun was bright and fresh, because his clothing seemed to work, he decided to hunt, and it was in this way that he found the moose.

Chapter

NINE

He prepared for hunting by putting his hatchet and knife on his belt and one of the butane lighters in his pocket. He started to take the light bow but thought that he might see something big and want to take a shot and so took the war bow under the theory that he could shoot something small with the big bow but he couldn't shoot a deer with the small bow. So he took the large bow and the new lance and five arrows with stone points and went hunting.

At the start he almost couldn't hunt. The woods were so beautiful, so changed—it was a whole different world—that he walked slowly along and feasted his eyes on first one scene and then another. It should all be framed, he thought—framed in some way to take back.

Take back. He hadn't thought that in a long while either. Pictures of home were fading. But if he could show this to his mother, he thought, just for her to *see* this . . .

He shook his head and almost at the same instant saw a rabbit. It was sitting under an overhanging evergreen limb, back in the shadow, but still very easy to see because it was brown. On its back there were several white spots, each about as large as a silver dollar. Brian had seen several rabbits with similar white spots and had thought they were some kind of fluke or mutation but he guessed now that they actually changed color in the winter and became white so that they wouldn't be so visible.

Without it, Brian thought, they were dead meat. A week or so earlier he had walked through and seen one rabbit in this area. He now took twenty steps and saw seven, all at varying ranges, none close enough to shoot, all standing out like sore thumbs because they were brown against the white snow.

He moved easily, slowly, waiting for a close shot. When it came—a rabbit not more than twenty feet away—he shot carefully and only missed by a hair, actually cutting the fur along the top of the rabbit's shoulders. The rabbit dodged left, then right, and vanished in the underbrush and Brian went forward to get his arrow.

At first he couldn't find it. He'd seen it fly, had seen exactly where it went into the snow—there was a hole marking the arrow's entry—but it wasn't there. He dug in the snow but still couldn't find it and didn't find it until he'd stepped back and lined up the flight of the arrow and worked along the snow scooping it out every foot. The arrow had gone more than thirty feet *after* entering the snow, skittering along beneath the surface before coming to rest. He'd have to be careful of his shots, he thought, pulling it out and blowing the snow off the feathers—he'd lose all his arrows on one hunt.

He moved on, still taken by the beauty, and had three more shots, all of which he missed because the targets were so small—rabbits—and he wasn't used to shooting the heavier bow yet.

I'll have to get closer, he thought—work right up on them, get into the thicker brush.

He slowed his pace even more and moved into a large stand of brambles and thick young evergreens, packed so closely he couldn't see more than ten feet, and that only by crouching down and looking along the ground. It was hard going. Every limb pulled at the bow and he had to be careful not to wreck the feathers on the arrows as he moved.

There were rabbits everywhere. The snow was covered with their tracks and he had moved nearly fifty yards into the thick brush when the sound of a breaking limb stopped him cold. Rabbits and foolbirds did not break limbs when they moved. Deer broke limbs, bear broke limbs.

Almost simultaneously he saw different tracks in the snow in front of him. Big tracks. Huge tracks. The hair went up on his neck. They were big enough for bear and what he really didn't want to do in his whole life was meet a bear in thick brush, especially if it was a bear that had a memory of a bad night with a skunk.

But when he leaned down to study the tracks he saw they had a cloven hoof, like those left by deer but larger. Much larger.

Moose. He knew instantly. He had seen moose several times since he had been attacked last summer. Once he had seen a bull with a rack so large that Brian could easily have fit between the antlers; the rest had been cows. They were all unbelievably big, and after he'd been attacked by the cow along the lake he'd given them a wide berth. When they got angry it was like having a Buick mad at you.

But, he thought—just that at first. But.

But what? But the moose are smaller now? But I'm tougher now? He shook his head, pushed the thoughts away, the sneaky thoughts, the ones that said he was hunting meat for food, moose were made out of meat, he had a larger bow, primitive people hunted moose with weapons like his, he *was* different now.

He heard the sound again. A breaking limb. Close, maybe thirty yards, and he crouched down and looked along the snow as he had for rabbits.

There. A brown leg moving, then another, like small trees they were, suddenly moving small trees.

He held his breath and crouched, watching. He could not see more of the moose, just the legs, and as he watched they moved off to the left a bit, hesitated, then turned left again and started moving slowly.

Directly at him.

Ahh, he thought. There it is—like it or not I am about to hunt moose. His stomach tightened and he stood and quickly glanced at his position. The brush was too thick for him to run even if he had wanted to and the truth was he didn't want to. He *was* different, he *did* have better weapons—and there was a lot of meat on a moose.

No room, he thought, to maneuver or to shoot. He

moved his head to the right and all he could see was thick brush, then to the left, and it was the same.

No. There, a small opening. Not four feet across and about four feet off the ground—almost a tunnel through the brush—but if it all worked right, all worked exactly right, he might be able to get a shot.

He moved to the left and stood facing the opening, leaned the killing lance against a nearby bush, held the bow up—with the top tipped slightly to the right to keep it out of the brush—and put his best arrow on the string ready to draw and waited.

And waited.

Time seemed to stop.

Somewhere to his left he heard the soft sound of a bird's wings, then the scratchy sound of a chickadee.

Brush cracked directly in front of him but he could see nothing.

Another bird flew past.

He aged, waiting, and now he heard the moose stepping, its hooves shussh-shusshing in the snow, and another breaking branch and then a line, a curved line as the side of the moose's front end came into view in the tunnel.

Brian tensed, his fingers tightening on the string. The edge of the shoulder moved slowly, ever so slowly to the left, bringing more and more of the moose's chest into view.

A third there, then a half, then two thirds and then the whole chest.

Brian drew the shaft back.

A cow, his brain registered, a large cow moose. No ant-lers. A little spit dripping from the side of her mouth. Brown eyes looking at him but not seeing him, or at least he hoped not.

Twenty feet, no more. Six, seven paces at the most.

He released the bowstring.

He could see it all later in his mind's eye so it all must have registered but when he did it everything happened so fast—and yet incredibly slowly—that it all seemed one event.

The arrow jumped from the string and he saw the feath-ers fly straight away from him and at the moose and slam into the moose's neck just above the center of her chest and in that instant, in the same split second, the moose caught the movement of the bow and arrow and Brian's head and charged, so fast she almost met the arrow.

If Brian had expected the brush to slow her down, or the arrow striking her to handicap her, he was sadly mistaken. She was at him like a cat, so fast that she seemed a blur, and yet his mind took it all in.

I hit her. The arrow hit her in the neck. She's charging. She's charging at me. Another arrow. No, no time. The lance. That's it, the lance.

He threw the bow aside and reached for the lance, all in one motion and all too late. He felt his hand clamp on the shaft of the lance and at the same time she came out of the brush on top of him. He had one fleeting image of a wall of brown hair with the feathers of the arrow sticking out of the middle and he went down.

He would never know what saved him. She was gigantic and on him and he thought she would crush him, mash him into the ground. But either the arrow hampered her movement or her momentum carried her too far and she went on over Brian and had to turn and come back at him.

He was hurt. His leg, his shoulder, yet he could move, and he rolled, still holding the killing lance, and came up to a kneeling position. He raised the head of the lance just as she hit him again.

One image. She threw herself at him, her eyes red with rage, and he saw her run onto the lance, the point entering her chest just below the arrow. Then her head hit his forehead. Brian saw one flash of white light, as bright as all the snow, then nothing but pain and darkness.

Chapter

TEN

A great weight. Something heavy on him. His mother was calling for him to come back. He was little again, a small boy and playing outside, and his mother was calling for him to come inside but he couldn't move because there was a huge weight on him, holding him down, keeping him from coming home . . .

Brian opened his eyes slowly, closed them against the brightness and the pain in his forehead, then opened them again.

It was, he thought, the same world. Snow all around, bright sun, he was breathing, had a pounding pain in his forehead—it reminded him of the plane crash—and had what appeared to be an entire cow moose in his lap.

He twitched when he looked down at her. Her eyes still looked mad, and her head plowed against his chest. But he realized she was dead. He started to examine his own situation.

Nothing seemed to be broken. He could not at first believe this and moved his arms and legs several times to make certain, then squirmed his way out from beneath the moose. She was lying half on him, her head on his chest pushing him back, and when he stood it was the first time he got a long look at how big she was.

From nose to back end he guessed a good eight or nine feet, maybe more. He paced her off and came up with four paces in length, counting her legs, which were sticking out a bit.

Maybe ten feet. And she was taller at the shoulder than he stood.

He wondered for a moment if she was the same moose that had attacked him earlier in the summer and tried to feel that she was, tried to feel some animosity toward her. But the truth was that killing her made him sad—elated and sad all at once, as he had been with the wolf-killed doe.

She was ugly and beautiful at the same time, lying there in the snow, blood from her chest wounds smeared where she lay—an ugly beautiful animal, and she was ended now. He had killed her, ended her life so that he could live, and he felt as bad as he felt good.

He turned away for a moment, shook his head and then turned back. There was much work to do and for a moment he thought it would be impossible. It was perhaps half a mile back to camp and there was absolutely no way he would be able to drag her.

He tried lifting a back leg and it was all he could do to get it off the ground. Dragging her would be simply impossible. She must weigh six or seven hundred pounds.

He would have to cut her up here and take her back to camp in pieces and that nearly stopped him. How, he thought, do you cut a moose up? Never in all his life had he *ever* thought about cutting a moose to pieces. Where did he start? There were no dotted lines the way there were in the diagram at the meat market . . .

He thought on it a full five minutes, looking at her lying there, and finally realized he could do nothing until she was skinned.

He used the knife to slit the hide from the neck, down the chest and belly to the back end. He had to cut around the lance—which had broken off after driving into her—and the arrow shaft still sticking out because they wouldn't pull free.

The skin came away harder than with the doe, was thicker and had to be cut loose as he skinned, peeling it back a half inch at a time all along her body. When he cut along the belly the knife slipped and cut the membrane holding the stomach in and her guts fell out on his feet, steaming, and he went ahead and pulled them the rest of the way out, amazed at how much there was inside her. The liver alone weighed more than two rabbits and he set it aside to cook later.

With the guts out of her she was easier to move—still very hard, but some easier—and he quickly developed a rhythm for skinning. Pull on the hide, slide the knife along, pull, slide, pull, slide. In half an hour he had lifted the hide completely off her right side, cutting it around the neck just under her head, and folded it over her back, completely exposing her right side.

He had never, even in a butcher shop, seen so much

meat in one place. She was a house of meat. Again he lifted the back leg and couldn't move her, even with the guts out. But as he lifted the leg he noted that there seemed to be a seam where the leg joined the body, a junction, and he put the knife there and cut and the leg lifted away from the body.

He kept lifting and cutting, all around the top of the back leg, pushing up as he did so until it was joined only at the hip socket, which rotated freely, and he cut around the socket with the knife, and it popped loose and the leg lifted completely away.

Just that, her back leg, was heavier than the doe, and he realized it would be hard to get the leg back to the shelter.

This would be a long job. He decided to pull the leg back and then return to finish up. An all-night job. And it would be cold.

He took off with the leg and used nearly twenty minutes just to pull it to the shelter and was almost exhausted when he got there. He stored it along the wall and went back to where the body of the cow lay.

It was now midday and he was starving. He took fifteen minutes to gather wood and start a fire near the carcass and when it was blazing well he cut a strip of meat from the rump near where he'd lifted the leg off and hung it over a stick so that it was nearly in the flames.

He went back to cutting and skinning while it cooked. He cut away the right front shoulder—it lifted off much the same as the rear leg, the shoulder blade cutting away, and then the leg, and he dragged it back to camp and when he returned, the meat on the stick was perfect: burned a little on the outside and cooked clear through.

He cut pieces off and ate it standing there, looking down at the rest of the cow, and he thought he'd never tasted meat so good. It was better than deer or rabbit or foolbirds, better than beef. And there was fat on it, more fat than the doe had, and he craved fat, ate one piece of fat alone that was hanging on the side of the meat and had cooked separately and still craved it. He cut two large pieces of fat off the carcass and hung them over the fire to cook while he went back to work.

With the right legs gone she was lighter and by lifting the legs on the ground he found he could just roll her over to get at the uncompleted side.

Once she was over he skinned the side as he'd done the first one, working up to the back after cutting around the legs until the hide was completely free of the carcass. Then he cut the legs loose, dragged them one at a time back to camp and returned to the body of the moose in darkness.

Finding his way was no problem because there was a half-moon and it lighted the snow into something close to daylight. But the cold came now and he had no gloves. His hands chilled as he worked on the damp meat and he had to warm them over the fire often, which slowed him, and by midnight everything in him screamed to stop.

But the cow was a treasure house of food and hide and he wasn't about to leave her for the wolves, or the bear if it came along again. So he kept working.

With the legs and rump gone the remaining part of the

carcass was not too hard to handle. He used the hatchet to chop through the spine in two places and separated the back, middle and front end and it amazed him how much all animals were alike. She was immense, but the cow was built almost like a rabbit, with the same basic layout.

The same design, he thought, grinning, and supposed if he were on all fours he would look the same.

He cut her head away with the hatchet and dragged the front section of her body, the rib cage and the hump meat on top of her shoulders with it, back to the camp and then the rear end and the center at the same time.

That left only the hide and head. The head he could come back for tomorrow and he set off with the hide at probably four in the morning.

It was the worst. It was staggeringly heavy—he couldn't lift it—and dragging it back to camp, with his bow and arrows on top of it, exhausted him.

At camp he looked at the pile of meat and hide next to his shelter wall, smiled once, shucked out of his rabbit-skin shirt, crawled into his bag and was in a deep, dreamless sleep in seconds.

A good—no, he thought, his brain closing down, a great day. A meat day. A moose day. He would sketch it on the shelter wall tomorrow . . .

Chapter

ELEVEN

The cow proved to be a godsend. The next day Brian awakened in midafternoon starving and not sure it had all happened—although his body felt as if he'd been sleeping in a cement mixer. Every bone and muscle seemed to ache. But the moose was all there, leaning against the side of the shelter.

He was starving and made a fire outside. He used the hatchet to chop out a section of ribs and cooked them on a stick over the flames and ate them when the fat was crackling.

"All I need is some barbecue sauce," he said aloud, grease dripping down his chin. "And a Coke . . ."

When he had first come out of the shelter it had been partly cloudy with the sun shining through gray wisps of clouds, but while he ate, the clouds became thicker until there was no blue and he felt a few drops hit his cheek.

"Not again—not rain . . ."

But it was. It didn't pour at first and he took the rest of the day to get in firewood—he had found a stand of dead poplar, all dry and easy to burn but still about a half mile away, and he dragged wood until it was dark and the rain was a steady, miserable, cold downpour.

He made a fire inside the shelter with coals from the outside fire and soon it was warm and toasty. He hung the rabbit-skin shirt up to dry and lay back to wait the rain out. Having worked all night the previous night and slept most of the day, he wasn't sleepy and thought that the rain seemed light and would probably end by daylight and when he finally dozed off, warm and snug in the shelter, it seemed to be coming down more lightly all the time.

But at daylight it hadn't stopped. He looked out at the drizzle—it had melted all the snow off and everything was a mess and now it had become cold and the rain was freezing into ice on the limbs and grass and he was glad that he had plenty of wood pulled up and a dry place to live.

It rained for a solid eight days, cold and wet, and if he hadn't had the shelter and meat he would have gone crazy.

And in a strange way it never really did stop raining. Each day it got colder and colder and the rain kept coming down and Brian could hear limbs breaking off with the weight of the ice on them and just when he thought he could stand it no longer the rain turned to snow.

Only this time not a soft snow. A wind came out of the northwest that howled through the trees like something insane, actually awakened him in the middle of the night and made him sit bolt upright in fear.

The snow was small and hard at first, driven needles that seemed to cut his cheek when he looked outside, and then changing to blown finer snow that found ways to seep into the shelter and melt hissing on the fire.

He was not idle. He had dragged in enough wood to

last if he was careful, but by the second and third day he was going stir-crazy and was looking for things to do.

Luckily there was much that needed doing. His clothing was far from adequate. The rabbit-skin shirt was like paper and ripped easily—indeed had been torn in several places during the moose attack and needed restitching—and Brian, with great effort, stretched the moose hide out in the rain and cut it in half and brought the rear half into the shelter.

The hide was still wet from being on the moose, hadn't had time to dry, but the fire and heat in the shelter worked fast and within a few days it had dried sufficiently to work.

It was stiff and thick and while it was still damp he cut a rectangle for a moose shirt, stitching it down the sides with moose-hide laces, making it larger than the rabbit-skin shirt. He did the same kind of sleeves and then made a crude hood, which he stitched around the head opening.

He did all this with the hair side in and when he put the rabbit-skin shirt on underneath and then the moose-hide parka on the outside—even with the moose hide still un-cured—he could feel his body warming up instantly.

He also nearly went down with the weight. He figured the coat weighed at least thirty pounds, maybe more, and decided he wouldn't be doing much running in it.

The snowstorm lasted three days on top of the rain and Brian worked on his weak spot—his hands. He used moose hide and made a pair of crude mittens by using his hands for a pattern and a piece of charcoal to draw on the hide. The thumbs were so large he could almost stick his whole hand in the thumbhole. These he made with the hair side in and fashioned them large enough to allow a second set of rabbit-skin mitts to be worn inside. The mittens were so big they kept falling off his hands and he used moose hide to make a cord that went over his shoulders and held the mittens up if he relaxed his hands.

This was all hard work and kept him busy for days, but worse work was the hide. As it dried it started to harden and it turned into something very close to a board.

He worked it back and forth over a rounded piece of wood as he'd done with the lacing and this process, trying to soften the dried moose hide, took longer than sewing up the clothing. And in the end he had to settle for less than he wanted. He had the hide loose where it counted, in the armpits and elbows and the hood, but much of the rest of it was only half supple, stiff enough so that he felt as if he were wearing a coat of armor and still stiff though he worked on it for hours when at last the storm ended.

Brian expected to be snowed in but in fact it was only eight or nine inches deep. It had been a fine, driven snow and hadn't accumulated to any depth but it was blasted into everything. Many of the trees had a full six inches sticking out to the *side* of the tree, where the snow had been driven by the wind.

It was still beautiful in the sunlight but had a different look from the last, fluffy snow, and it was cold, a deeper cold than before.

Brian couldn't estimate temperature but he thought it must be near zero, but quiet—the wind had stopped completely—and his clothes kept him as warm as if he'd been in the shelter.

He started to brush the snow off the stacked moose meat and then thought better of it. The meat was frozen and protected under the snow and ice from the rain and safer there than in the open. He didn't think the bear would come—it must be hibernating by now, and the same for Betty, whom he hadn't seen since just after the bear attack—so the meat should be all right just beneath the snow.

He needed wood and he spent most of that day dragging in dead poplar, finally taking the parka off because it was so heavy and working in the rabbit-skin shirt alone. Everything had ice frozen on it but it chipped off easily with the hatchet. When he had a good stack—enough for another week (he was definitely gun-shy now about storms)—he chopped some meat off one of the back legs of the moose for stew and settled in for another night of rubbing the hide of his parka to soften it.

And he wondered that night—the night of day ninety-four—if this was it; was this all winter would be? Eating meat and rubbing hide and waiting for the next rain to turn to snow?

TWELVE

It did not rain again.

Nor did the snow go away. The temperature stayed down and in four days it snowed lightly, maybe an inch, and then in four more days another inch or two and then in four more days . . .

Regular as clockwork winter came. The snow never came deeply, never another wild blizzard, just an inch or two every four days. But the snow didn't leave between times, didn't melt, and before long there was a foot on the ground, a foot of dry powder.

At first it was all very settled and comfortable. Brian's clothing seemed to work, he had plenty of meat and plenty of firewood—although he had to go some distance to get it. He knew how much wood it would take for a given time and brought in enough for a week—it took a full day—and then had nothing to do the rest of the week except work his moose-hide clothing against the wooden peg to soften it and eat moose-meat stew.

Summer had been so active and now he had suddenly come to a virtual stop. He couldn't fish anymore because the ice was too thick to chop through with the hatchet, he didn't need to hunt because he had—he figured roughly—

four hundred pounds of moose left to eat. Lying by the fire one evening softening hide, he did some rough math, and if he ate four pounds of moose meat a day he would make at least a hundred days before needing more meat. More than three months. Let's see, he thought, it was late November now, no, early December, no, wait . . .

He counted the days on his marks and decided it was the last week in November. Thanksgiving—he'd forgotten Thanksgiving.

He could do that. Have a Thanksgiving meal. The date was a little off, he would be late, but it felt good to think of it and he prepared for it as if he were home.

He would eat moose, of course, but he had found that the hump meat was the best and he chopped a three-pound piece off the frozen block by his door.

He would need more—some kind of sauce.

Then he remembered the berries. On one of his wood-gathering runs he'd gone past the north end of the lake and there had been a string of small, scraggly trees loaded with bright red berries. Because everything was under a foot of snow and he hadn't seen a berry since summer these berries—looking fresh and bright even though they were frozen solid—struck him as very odd. They looked delicious and hung in small clumps and he smelled them, then took a handful and popped them into his mouth.

At first he couldn't taste them because they were frozen but as soon as they thawed he got the flavor. They were tangy and had a mild bitter taste that made him want to pucker—also they had large pits. They were similar to the gut cherries he'd had trouble with during the summer except that they didn't make him sick and the sour taste reminded him of something else he couldn't at first place and later remembered as a vinegar or sour sauce flavor.

They would make a good sauce for a Thanksgiving meal and he went along the lakeshore and picked one of the smaller aluminum pans full and it was in this way that he learned about snowshoes.

It did not come that fast. There was about a foot of snow, powder but with a stiffness, and as he walked along the lake in his deer-hide boots he startled a rabbit from beneath an evergreen and it took off like a shot—all changed to white—across the snow.

Without sinking in. Brian watched it run away and had taken another four or five steps when it hit him that the rabbit was running on *top* of the snow while Brian was sinking in with each step.

He moved to the rabbit's tracks and studied them. They were huge, fully twice the size of the feet he had seen on rabbits earlier, and when he examined the tracks more closely he saw that the rabbit had grown hair to increase the size of its feet and he thought how perfect they were: to be able to do that, change color in the winter and grow bigger feet to stay on top of the snow. How perfect. And he set the information back in his mind and went on about preparing for Thanksgiving.

He packed snow in with the berries and put them on the fire to melt and boil; then he put the hump meat in the large pan with snow and set that on to boil as well.

So much, he thought, for cooking Thanksgiving dinner.

What he wanted was a table and a chair and a table-cloth—no, he thought. What he wanted was a turkey and all the trimmings and then a table and chairs and tablecloth and his mother and father sitting with him and milk, oh yes, a glass of cold milk and bread and butter and potatoes and gravy and . . .

What he wanted more than anything was out, to be back in the world. To have all that stuff and be back in the world and then to go to a movie, no, to sit and watch television with your belly packed and watch a football game and belch and . . .

That was what he wanted.

What he did instead was clean his shelter.

He had been sleeping on the foam pad that had come with the survival pack and he straightened everything up and hung his bag out in the sun to air-dry and then used the hatchet to cut the ends of new evergreen boughs and laid them like a carpet in the shelter.

As soon as he brought the boughs inside and the heat from the fire warmed them they gave off the most wonderful smell, filled the whole shelter with the odor of spring, and he brought the bag back inside and spread the pad and bag and felt as if he were in a new home.

The berries boiled first and he added snow water to them and kept them boiling until he had a kind of mush in the pan. By that time the meat had cooked and he set it off to the side and tasted the berry mush.

Bitter, he thought, but tangy and not all that bad, and

he cut a piece of the moose hump off, a thin slice, and dipped it in the sauce and ate it in two bites.

It was delicious, almost like having steak sauce or a kind of bitter catsup. He took another cut of meat, dipped it, ate it as well, the juice dripping down his chin, and was on his third one when he realized this was his Thanksgiving dinner.

And I'm eating like a wolf, he thought, before I give thanks.

It stopped him, the idea of giving thanks. At first his mind just stopped and he thought, for what? For the plane crash, for being here? I should thank somebody for that?

Then a small voice, almost a whisper, came into his mind and all it said was: It could have been worse; you could have been down in the plane with the pilot.

And he felt awful for his attitude, turned away from the food and forced himself to be grateful for all the good luck he'd had and to not think about the bad at all.

Just that, escaping from the plane alive—that was luck. And to be able to live and learn and know things, to be able to hunt, to be thankful for the animals' lives that had been spent to keep him fed, to be thankful for the deer and the moose, lord, the moose like getting a whole food store and to be thankful for his shelter and knife and the hatchet . . .

The hatchet. The key to it all. Nothing without the hatchet. Just that would take all his thanks.

And every stick, every twig of wood that burned to keep him warm and his sleeping bag and Betty saving him from the bear and the chickadees that hung around the camp and the sun that brought each new day . . .

All that, he thought, all that and more to be thankful for and he ended the prayer—as it had seemed to become—with another thought about the pilot down in the lake, how he hoped the pilot had had a good life and was where it was good for him now.

Then he ate, quietly, thinking of his mother and father, and when he finished his Thanksgiving it was dark, pitch-dark, and he crawled into his bag to sleep and had just closed his eyes and started to get drowsy when he heard the gunshot.

Chapter

THIRTEEN

It did not register at first.

The night had grown very cold and still and the shelter was warm and he was in that state just between waking and sleeping when he heard a sharp, blistering crack of sound.

He was half dreaming and thought it was part of the dream but it cracked again, a little more away and then a third time, very far away.

By the third shot he was on his feet and had pushed the door away and was standing in the opening.

"Hey! Over here, I'm over here!"

He listened and heard two other, much more muted shots and then nothing. Since he slept with no pants and his underwear had long since given up the ghost he was standing nude in the cold air. For a second or two his body heat held but then it started down fast and he felt the cold come into him.

Still he stood, listening, holding his breath, and he heard one more pop, so far away it could hardly be heard and after that no further sound.

"Hey!" he yelled one more time but there was no answer and the cold was getting to him so he closed the door and climbed back into the bag.

It was insane. All that shooting in the dark—who was doing it? And what were they shooting at? He would have to go out tomorrow and look for tracks, at least where the nearest shot seemed to come from—somewhere just across the lake.

And why didn't they answer him? They must have heard him—what was the matter with them? Was it some maniac? And why hadn't Brian seen him, or heard him before . . .

He meant to sleep, was tired enough to sleep, but he could not get the image out of his mind—some crazy man with a high-powered rifle was out there somewhere, shooting at things in the dark.

So Brian put a little more wood on the fire and blew on the coals to get it going and sat all night, dozing intermittently, waiting for daylight so that he could look for tracks.

At first light he got into his clothing and slid the door open and stepped outside.

Into a wall of cold.

He had read about cold—a teacher had read poems to him about Alaska when he was small—and heard stories and seen shows on the Discovery Channel on television but he had never felt anything like this.

His breath stopped in his throat. It felt as if the moisture on his eyes would freeze and he did feel the lining of his nose tighten and freeze. There was no wind, not even a dawn breeze—it was absolutely still—and when he took a step forward he felt the air moving against his eyes and he had to blink to keep them from freezing.

Thirty, forty, fifty below—he couldn't even guess how

cold it was—and he thought, This is how people die, in this cold. They stop and everything freezes and they die.

He pulled his hood up and was surprised, crude as it was, at how much it increased the warmth around his head. Then he pulled the mittens on and picked up his killing lance—long since repaired from the moose kill—and moved forward and as soon as he moved he felt warmer.

The snow was dry, like crystallized flour or sugar, and seemed to flow away from his legs as he walked.

He made a circle of the camp, walked out on the lake ice—which was covered with snow as well—and back around and saw no tracks other than rabbit and mouse.

Then he started to move toward where the sound had come from, working slowly, amazed that he was starting to warm up and even feel comfortable. Back in the hood the air was kept from moving and his face grew warmer and the fact that his head was warm seemed to warm his whole body and once he became accustomed to the cold he could look around and appreciate the world around him.

It was a world of beauty. It's like being inside glass, he thought, a beautiful glass crystal. The air was so clear he could see tiny twigs, needles on pine trees fifty, seventy-five yards away, and so still that when a chickadee flew from a tree to the meat piled near the entrance—where they flocked and picked at the meat—he could actually hear the rush of air as the bird flapped its wings.

Tracks went everywhere. Once he was in the woods away from camp there were so many rabbit prints he felt there must be hundreds of them just living around the shelter. The tracks were so thick in some places that they had formed packed trails where the rabbits had run over the same place until it became a narrow highway. Some of the snow was packed so densely that it would hold Brian up and he walked single file on the tracks, where the brush permitted, to keep from sinking into the snow.

But he wasn't looking for rabbit tracks. Somebody had been out there firing a gun and it hadn't snowed during the night so there should be tracks, had to be tracks.

But there were none. He moved farther out from the camp, circled again, making wide arcs in the direction the sound had come from, and there were no tracks—or none other than mice, deer, something he thought was a fox, and about a million rabbits.

He stopped at midday and stood by a tree trying to find some other sign, something that would tell him how they did it . . .

Had he dreamed the whole thing? Could he have been dreaming of gunshots? Or maybe he'd been alone too much and was going insane. That could happen. It happened all the time. People went crazy under far less stress than Brian had been under. Maybe that was it—he'd dreamed it or had finally gone insane. Sure . . .

Craaack!

It was near his head and he dropped to his knees. They were shooting at him. And they were close, right next to him. No dream this time, no insanity—they were right on top of him.

He rolled to his left and came up in a crouch behind a

large pine, waiting, watching. Nothing—he could see absolutely nothing out of the ordinary. Just brush and trees and . . . there. He had been looking along the ground and he brought his eyes up a bit, so that they were scanning ten feet up, and he saw it.

A poplar tree was shattered; bits of wood and bark seemed to have been blown out of it as if it had been hit by an exploding shell. It was still standing but was severely damaged and he thought for a moment that somebody was playing pranks, shooting a tree ten feet off the ground.

But it hadn't been shot. He moved closer to the tree and studied it and there was no evident bullet hole—just the shattering wound—and it is likely he would never have known except that he actually saw it happen and it was almost the last thing he saw happen on earth.

Directly in front of him, not fifteen feet away and just slightly higher than his head, a footlong section of tree exploded with a shattering, cracking sound that nearly deafened him and at the same time a sliver of wood from the tree came at him like an arrow. There was no time to dodge, move, even blink. The sliver—a foot long and slightly bigger in diameter than his thumb and sharp as a needle—came at his face, brushed violently past his ear and stuck halfway out the back of the leather hood.

He reached up to grab the sliver with his mittens on, couldn't because they were too bulky and threw the right one off and grabbed the wood with his bare hand.

It was frozen solid, so cold that it stuck to the warm skin on his fingers and he had to shake it off. The tree was frozen all the way through. It was strange but he'd never thought of it, never considered what happened to trees when it got cold. He just figured they got through it somehow—they just got cold.

But there was moisture in them, sap, and when it got very cold the sap must freeze. He went up to the tree that had just exploded and saw that a whole section seemed to have been blown out of the side—maybe a foot and a half long and four or five inches wide. Just shattered and blown apart and the force seemed to have come from inside the tree and he stood back and stared at the wound and thought on it and finally came up with a theory.

The tree would freeze on the outside first, a ring of frozen wood all the way around. Then, when it got truly cold—as it had last night—the inside would freeze. When liquid freezes it expands—he had learned that in Ms. Clammon's science class—or tries to expand. But with the wood frozen all around it there was no space for the center to expand. It simply stayed there, locked in the center while the outside held it in and the containment forced the center to build up pressure, and more pressure and still more, until it couldn't be contained and blew out the side of the tree.

It wasn't gunshots. It was trees exploding. There were no crazy people running around with guns and Brian hadn't gone off the deep end.

It was just winter, that was all. Brian stared at the tree and then around the woods and knew one thing now for a certainty: Everything was different. The woods in summer

102

were a certain way and now they were a different way, a completely different place.

And if he was to stay alive he would have to learn this new place, this winter woods. He would have to study it and know it. The next time he might not be so lucky . . .

Chapter

FOURTEEN

It proved to be much harder than he had thought it would be. That night a front came in and the temperature rose—a welcome relief—to probably an even zero, and it snowed. This time it snowed close to six inches and while that would not have been so bad in itself it came on top of snow that was already there. All in all it added up to just under two feet of snow, dry powder, and when he tried to move in the woods it was too much. It came over the top of his cylinder boots and froze his legs and he had to go back to the shelter to get rid of the snow and dry his boots out.

"This," he said, sitting by the fire, "is as bad as it gets . . ."

The truth was, it could be fatal. He needed to move in the woods to get firewood—not to mention hunting and studying to learn—and if he could not move without freezing his feet he could not get wood and without wood he would freeze to death.

It seemed to be a wall. He sat, burning the last two days' worth of wood, and felt the cold waiting, waiting. Dark came suddenly at four in the afternoon and he sat in the dark for a while and thought on the problem and was leaning back gazing into the fire when he remembered the rabbits.

They grew larger feet.

He had to do the same. As soon as he thought it he smiled and thought of snowshoes. They had completely slipped his mind.

All he had to do was make a pair of snowshoes.

I'll get right on it tomorrow morning, he thought, lying back to doze in his bag, and was nearly asleep, smiling in comfort and ease now that he had solved the problem, when he realized that he didn't have the slightest idea how to make a pair of snowshoes.

It kept him awake for another hour, until he simply couldn't keep his eyes open any longer, and then he fell asleep without a solution.

Two bows.

It came in the half sleep just before he awakened. It was cold, the fire was burned down, and he felt snug and warm in the bag and didn't want to get up, and lay with his eyes closed, his head tucked down inside the bag, and dozed, and was almost back asleep when the thought hit him.

Two bows.

If he made two bows of wood, then tied the ends together, used some kind of crosspieces to hold them apart and keep them in a rough oval, he would have the right shape for snowshoes.

And it proved to be almost that easy. He cut wood from

the willows down by the lake and brought four five-foot-long pieces into the shelter where it was warm, along with some other shorter sections he'd cut from the lower and thicker branches on the same willow.

They were frozen solid but they thawed quickly by the fire and were as limber as they had been in the summer. He peeled the bark from them easily with the knife and then took two of them and tied the ends together with moose-hide lacing. After they were tied together he pulled the center sections apart until he could put the hatchet between them to hold them apart—about twelve inches—and then he used the knife to cut crosspieces and notch the ends of the shorter sections to fit around the wood of the long side and make cross-braces.

He put two cross-braces to hold the long sides apart and then tied the cross-braces in place with strips of moose-hide lacing and had the frame for a snowshoe.

He made a second one the same way—all of this didn't take two hours—and moved on to the next step.

He would have to fill them with lacing and there was plenty of moose hide left but it was frozen outside. He brought it inside and let it thaw near the fire for the rest of the afternoon until he could unfold it and start to cut lacing to make the web of the snowshoe.

Here it was all mystery to him. He had seen pictures of snowshoes and had a vague idea that they seemed to be a web, kind of like a tennis racket—a very crude tennis racket—but that was it.

He had plenty of moose hide left and he started by cutting a lace half an inch wide. He did not know how much he would need but figured it should be long so he just kept cutting, running along the edge of a large piece of hide, cutting around and around the edge, stopping often to sharpen the knife on the stone until he had a pile of lacing lying on the ground by the fire.

By this time it was dark but he fed small bits of wood to the fire—the shelter was very tight and stayed surprisingly warm from just a small flame—and continued working.

He did not know how to make the rest of the snowshoe. He had seen pictures and knew it had to be a web of some sort but could not visualize how to start. In the end he just started in the middle and worked to the ends, tying the strips of moose hide crosswise, fastened to each side, making horizontal strips about two inches apart, each strap pulled tight and tied off in a double knot.

The hide was hard and he had to soften it by rubbing it over a stick to break it down, which slowed him, and it was late by the time he'd finished the crosspieces on one shoe but instead of going to bed he continued.

The strips that ran the long way he tried simply weaving into place but they were too loose and so he tied them off to each cross-strap as he went from one end of the shoe to the other, again with the straps about two inches apart.

It was moving toward morning when he finished the webbing on one shoe and he almost laughed at how it looked. He had not taken the fur off the hide strips and there was enough hair to fill all the holes with fuzz. He started to burn it off and then realized it would help keep him up in soft snow. He finally crawled into his bed to sleep about four in the morning, still smiling at how the shoe looked.

He slept hard until daylight—about nine o'clock—and then kindled the fire and restarted it with the coals that were still glowing. He had chopped some chunks of moose meat and he put a kettle on with slivers of meat and snow to make a breakfast stew and as soon as the shelter was warm went back to work.

The second shoe went much faster because of the practice he'd had on the first one and by midday he had finished webbing it. He ate the stew and drank the broth and then looked once more at his handiwork.

They looked odd, to say the least—downright ugly. The fur was so thick he could hardly see the lacing. But they also looked strong and now all he had to do was find a way to fix them to his feet.

He could think of no mind pictures, no memories that showed snowshoe bindings, and finally he simply tied straps across down the middle, as tightly as possible, to jam his feet beneath.

Then there was nothing to do but try them. He banked the fire so that the coals would hold for a time, got dressed and took the shoes outside.

They were very tight on his boots and felt snug and he set off trying to walk on them at once. Around the shelter the snow was packed down where he had walked and the shoes were easy—clumsy, but he could skid them along.

As soon as he moved away from the shelter in fresh snow everything changed. He took two steps and fell flat on his face in the snow. The tips kept digging in and tripping him and he tried holding his toes up, which didn't help, and continued stumbling along, falling over frontward, until he thought of moving the foot strap forward a bit.

This just took a minute and then when he stepped off, his foot was farther forward and lifted the front of the shoe first, cleared the tip and pulled it across the top of the snow.

It made all the difference. He tripped twice more before he developed a pace that kept his legs far enough apart to prevent the shoes from hitting each other and then he moved into deeper snow.

It was amazing. The snow was powdery and the shoes didn't keep him right on top as he'd thought they might. But he only went down three or four inches and stopped, instead of his foot going all the way down into two feet of snow, and as an added benefit the snowshoes kept the snow away from his feet and legs.

He didn't get snow down his boots, his legs stayed warmer and dryer and that kept the rest of his body warmer and dryer but more, much more than that, he could *move* again.

He moved straight to a stand of dead poplar a quarter mile down the lakeshore. Poplars often died standing and for that reason stayed dry and out of the snow and were good firewood. He hadn't been able to get at them because of the snow but the shoes made it easy.

He broke off limbs and knocked over small dead trees and, walking with a kind of forward churning motion, he spent the rest of the day bringing in wood until he had a huge pile next to the shelter—enough for a week.

It was incredible, he thought, how the snowshoes seemed to change everything, change his whole attitude. He'd been closing down, he realized—settling into the shelter, not paying attention to things, getting more and more into his own thinking, and the shoes changed all that. He felt like moving, hunting, seeing things, doing things again.

Thinking of hunting brought his food supply into his thoughts and he brushed the snow away from the moose meat and was stunned to see how much he'd eaten. He hadn't gained weight, had lost a small amount as a matter of fact, and yet apparently without knowing it had been eating like a wolf.

He'd eaten both front shoulders, the back and hump area and one back leg—all the meat was chopped off the bones in those areas. All he really had left was the left rear leg and then chopping and boiling the bones to make the meat jelly-stew.

He would have to hunt again and that night he spent the hours until he slept making sure his war bow and big arrows were in shape, checking the lance and sharpening the hatchet and knife and retightening his snowshoes where they had become loose from gathering wood all day.

That night the temperature dropped like a stone, so that he heard trees exploding again, but he slept hard and down and tight in his shelter and dreamed of walking on white clouds . . .

Chapter

FIFTEEN

Everything had changed.

Somehow he had thought that it would be like normal hunting except colder and whiter but it wasn't—it all seemed a different world.

He made a breakfast stew and ate while it was still dark and didn't open the shelter until close to ten, when the sun was well up.

Brian had never felt such cold, never thought he would see it, never thought that if he *did* see such cold he would live through it. He had his hood up and had to breathe slowly in through his nose to warm the air so that it would not stop halfway down his throat.

It was colder than before, how cold he couldn't guess, but when he went to the bathroom some of his urine froze on the way to the ground and broke when it hit and he spit on a clear area of hard-packed snow and the spit bounced.

Still he did not feel cold. There was no wind, not a breath, and he soon warmed inside his parka as he walked and started to hunt.

He hadn't shot in a while and wanted to try some practice shots but knew he would lose the arrows beneath the snow. He settled for pulling the bow back a few times and flexing his muscles and found that because the parka was so bulky he had to lean forward a bit to let the bowstring clear his sleeve. Also he couldn't keep his mitten off for long or his hand would freeze, so he would have to have time to shake the mitten off before shooting.

Game was everywhere. They didn't seem to mind the cold and he saw rabbits all over the place. He could have shot several but the moose had spoiled him. There was so much food in the large animal and only the one death—it still bothered him to kill—and it seemed more proper in some way. He would have to kill perhaps a hundred and fifty rabbits to equal one moose . . .

As it happened he did not get a moose. He didn't even see a moose. He saw their tracks and they looked fresh but after following a moose track for more than a mile and seeing no moose and no change in the track he decided it was impossible to tell a fresh track from an old one in powdery snow. They all looked the same.

He was working back toward camp and had decided that he should start trying to hit rabbits when he saw the deer.

It was a buck with only one antler. Brian guessed the other one had gotten knocked off or had never grown. But the buck was good-sized for all that—nowhere near a moose, but large for a deer—and Brian studied the layout carefully.

Brian was on a small rise and the deer was slightly below, standing on the edge of a round frozen pond about fifty yards away—much too far for a shot. The deer was in snow up to its belly, biting the tops off small red willows, eating them slowly, but its ears swiveled constantly and Brian knew he could move no closer directly without being heard.

But down and to his left as he faced the deer there was a shallow depression that angled toward the buck—not quite a ditch yet deep enough to hide everything but his head as he moved and Brian, carefully raising and moving his snowshoes forward, slowly, a step at a time, only just clearing the snow, moved down the depression.

He watched the deer, only lifted his foot to move when the deer had its head down to bite a willow, a step, another step, slowly, so slowly, and in what seemed hours he'd moved sideways and fifteen yards closer.

Thirty-five yards. Still too far—twice too far.

Wait, another step while the deer ate, another wait, holding his breath, two steps, one, half a step . . .

Twenty yards.

Eighteen, sixteen, fifteen.

Fifteen long paces.

He had learned how to hunt, how to wait for the exact right moment and not waste his shot, and he eased his hand out of the mitten, let it hang on its cord, put his fingers to the string where the arrow lay and waited, frozen motionless.

The deer looked right at him, stared at him, then looked down, back up, stamped its right foot, looked at him again and, finally satisfied, turned to take another bite of willow.

It would not get better.

Brian raised the bow carefully, drew, looked to where the arrow would go, where he wanted it to be, and released.

There was a slight *thrum* of the string and the arrow leaped away from the bow. The deer heard the sound, had time to start to turn its head, and then the arrow disappeared into its side just to the rear of the shoulder.

Nothing happened.

Brian still stood, holding his breath, the bow still out in front of him.

The deer stood, staring at him, seeing him now, feeling the pain of the arrow that had gone into the top of its heart, but still staring and then settling, down on its front end slowly—as slowly as Brian had walked—then down with its back end and the head curving over to the back until the one antler rested on its shoulder and it died that way, looking back and up at the sky.

Forever, Brian thought. It took forever. With the moose there had been violence, the charge, his killing lance, but this . . .

This was a kind of murder.

I should have missed, he thought, still standing with the bow out in front of him. I should have raised my hand and the arrow would have gone up a bit and I would have missed, should have missed.

In hunting terms it was a perfect kill, and it made Brian feel perfectly awful. The deer had been eating, just eating, and hadn't known he was there and the arrow had taken it . . .

He shook his head. He had done what he had to do and it was finished; he had taken meat and it would be wrong now to waste it.

He moved to the dead buck. It was a large deer—before the moose he would have considered it huge—but he had learned much from handling the moose, and he gutted the deer and peeled the skin back from the belly up to the back on one side, then rolled it and skinned the other side until the hide was free.

There were chunks of yellow-white fat on the carcass and hanging on the skin as well and he left them attached for the moment. He had a lot of daylight left but there was much work to do as well and he started in cutting the legs free as he had with the moose, then chopping the back into pieces. Again he left the head intact and cut it free from the hide and set it up in the crotch of a tree. He still could not bring himself to look at the eyes, though they were clouded and dull.

When the deer was cut up he laid the skin out flat and put the two back legs on it. It was in his mind to use the skin as a carrying pack but it had lain flat until it was frozen and was as hard and flat as a board.

Or a sled, he thought, looking at it from a different angle. He stacked all the meat, with the heart and liver, on the skin, then grabbed it where the head had been attached and pulled hard.

It slid forward easily, so easily he nearly fell over backward. The buck had thick hair but it was all slanted to the back and when he pulled forward the hairs lay back and let it slide like a flat-bottom sled.

"Slick," he said aloud. "Really slick . . ."

He had planned on making several trips the mile and a half back to the camp but now it could all be done in one so he took his time, sliding the hide along behind the snowshoe tracks and getting back to the shelter well before dark.

"I am fat," he said, looking at all he had: the rest of the moose, all the firewood he had gathered, the shelter and now the deer. "I'm set. Now all I have to do is . . ."

He couldn't think of a word. He wanted to say "play," but he didn't think in terms of playing any longer. Or maybe it was that he considered it *all* play.

That night he splurged and didn't boil meat. Instead he cut a steak off the deer and broiled it on sticks over the fire. It wasn't perfect—the sticks burned and the meat fell into the fire twice and he lost all the juice in the flames and it smoked up the inside of the shelter so that he had to open the door to clear it out—but it was good. The fat had cooked and burned a little and he ate until he thought his stomach would burst.

During the night a change awakened him and he lay with his eyes open in the dark until he realized that a breeze had come up and that the temperature was rising and the hard-bite cold was gone and there would probably be some snow coming.

He didn't care. He missed summer and the short fall that had followed but in some ways he liked winter better.

He hadn't, he thought, smiling as he went to sleep, seen a mosquito in months . . .

Chapter

SIXTEEN

The weather warmed and he started to run the next day.

Not literally—it was all he could do to walk fast in the snowshoes—but in the sense that wolves run.

He decided to see more, be more and not spend all his time in the shelter just living between kills and looking out the door now and then.

He wanted more, and the snowshoes and some new confidence made him free. He took his war bow and lance, a deerskin quiver of arrows over his back, a propane lighter and enough meat for the day wrapped in a hanging pouch of deer hide, and ran the way wolves ran, coursed just to see what he could see.

He moved out from the shelter in gradual circles, discovering the land. The first few days he did not go far, had a slight concern about becoming lost, and then decided it didn't matter. He would always find his way back by the snowshoe tracks and even if they filled in and it took him some time to find his way home to the shelter in a very real sense he was *always* home now in the woods; with the bow and hatchet at his belt and the lighter to start a fire and snowshoes to keep him above the snow he had become a creature of winter. Home was where he stopped to have a fire and by the end of a week—the warm weather held, rising to thirty above during the day—he actually stayed out away from the shelter for a night and sat by a fire in his clothes, listening to wolves howling, seeing a thousand diamond eyes from the firelight glittering in the snow around the fire pit.

The next day it grew warmer still and he was working a ridge about four miles from camp hunting a moose. He had no intention of killing the moose but was hunting like a wolf—not always to kill, but to know, to see. He had seen the moose, a large bull with both antlers gone, earlier in the day and had locked onto his tracks and followed a quarter mile back, watching the moose through the trees as the moose nibbled on the same willow shoots Brian had seen the deer eating. They made it look so good he tried them but they tasted like wood to him and he spit them out.

The moose didn't know Brian was there and Brian studied him carefully, watching him eat and move. The moose was huge, enormous, twice as big as the cow Brian had killed or maybe larger still, and Brian doubted that even with a full draw and very sharp arrow he could get a shaft deep enough to kill him. Perhaps with the lance and a good solid lunge or by having the bull run on the spear as the cow had done . . .

He was thinking this way, watching the bull from beneath an overhanging pine branch about a hundred yards away, imagining how it would be and what he would have to do to get the moose if he ever wanted to try it, when he saw the wolf kill.

At first he didn't recognize what was coming. He saw the moose stiffen and turn his head, his huge ears alert and forward, and then in a shadow he saw a flash of gray, just a touch, moving across the rear of the moose.

Wolf. He just had time to think the word when he saw another gray shape swipe through the trees, again across the rear of the bull, and then two more as they came in to cut and dodge and it looked like seven or eight of them but he thought probably only four.

It was enough. The bull tried to fight. He slashed with his front hooves and kicked with his back, swinging and swiveling to meet the attackers, but they kept coming from the side in slashing attacks aimed at the bull's back legs and rear end. They pulled at the hamstrings, cut at the back legs until the bull couldn't stand and as he caved in and settled on his rear the wolves became frantic and started tearing at his rear end, opening the bull while he was still alive, ripping at the rear leg muscles and the anus, each bite opening the wound more until blood was all over the snow and the wolves were covered with it.

And they ate him that way. Pulling at his rear while he still lived, pulling his insides out while he tried to pull himself away with his front legs until he was at last too weak and fell forward. Still alive, still living while they ate him.

Brian wanted to not see it. He had thought killing with the arrows slow and bad but this—it was nothing like this.

The wolves were crazy with it, with the smell of blood and from the hot intestines they pulled from the living moose, and the bull took forever to die, never died but just kept sinking down and down while the wolves ate him alive.

Brian shuddered. He had seen the wolves before and had never felt fear. He had not thought they would ever attack him but if they did—if they came in like that and pulled him down.

He looked away, shook his head. They would not attack. They hadn't yet and they had had plenty of opportunities. They ate deer and moose and hopefully not boys.

But still, as Brian left them eating and moved quietly away, still he kept an arrow in the bow and his fingers on the string and kept looking over his shoulder back at them pulling at the bull and gorging on the warm meat and later that night in the shelter he sat by the fire and wondered how it could be so horrible—how nature could let an animal suffer the way the moose had suffered.

The wolves were just being natural and he understood the need to kill—he would himself die if he did not kill.

But so slowly . . .

He stared into the flames for a long time thinking of it and thought he would dream of it when he slept, but he didn't. Instead he dreamed of home, of sitting watching television with his mother and father, and when he awakened it was well past daylight—the latest he had slept in some time.

He went outside to the bathroom and the weather was so soft and warm he didn't need his parka—a warm day in

December—and he turned back to build a fire and boil meat when he heard two trees explode, some distance off, one pop and after a short pause another one.

Pop . . . pop.

And he had the fire going and the pot on with snow and meat set to boil when he realized what he had heard, or what he *hadn't* heard.

It was too warm for trees to explode.

Chapter

SEVENTEEN

He had fooled himself before. He had thought he heard planes when none were there, had imagined he saw people, had thought guns were going off when trees were exploding—all wrong.

And so now he thought of what it could be. If it wasn't trees exploding then what? He could think of nothing but a gun, unless somehow trees exploded when it got warm as well as when it was cold.

He had neglected camp and spent all the next day cleaning the shelter, bringing in more wood, retightening the snowshoes, checking the bowstring and sharpening the hatchet and knife. It was still warm so he put his sleeping bag out to air and somehow when he had done these things it was near dark and time to cook again and settle in for the night.

But he was not tired, and all the day, while he worked around camp, and then at dark when he made the fire and started to cook, all that time he kept listening for the sound again, knowing that it was warm and that it might not be trees, but not thinking past that, just listening, waiting. But he did not hear it again.

He lay awake looking at the coals, the warm glow lighting his face, and when his eyes closed he knew that the next day he would go and try to find the place where he had heard the popping sounds. He thought it must be a good distance—the sounds were faint—and he would probably find some plausible reason for the sound.

But he would look.

He had to look.

He awakened before dawn, made a small fire to cook stew and then prepared his gear. He had not forgotten the wolves and he saw to his lance and war bow and arrows, hung the hatchet and knife on a thong around his shoulder and left camp just after good light.

Brian knew it might be a wasted trip and he decided to swing past the wolf-killed moose. There had been four wolves but it was a large moose and there would probably be meat left over—if the wolves were gone.

He needn't have worried. The wolves had eaten off the rear end and up the middle and were gone but the back and front shoulders were intact and Brian made a mental note to swing around and start carrying meat back to the camp when he finished the search.

The warm weather had softened the snow surface and then it had refrozen during the night, so the snowshoes didn't sink in at all but rode along the top and Brian found it was almost like skating.

"If I had skis," he murmured, "I could fly . . ." And he wondered how hard it would be to make a pair of skis—whittle them out of wood. Almost impossible, but his mind stayed on it, thinking on how he would cut a straight log and split it with the hatchet and carve it flat and somehow warp up the end, seeing it in his mind, visualizing each step, and he was so caught up in the idea of the skis that he almost missed it.

A line.

He had come three miles and a bit more, working along the tops of ridges where he could see farther. There were hundreds of ponds and lakes scattered through the woods and he wove between them, staying high. He saw three moose, more than a dozen deer and hundreds of rabbits and could have had many shots, but was trying to find some sign, something that would be out of the ordinary, and there it was:

A line.

In the middle of a lake more than a mile away and below the ridge he was walking on, out across the ice from the east to the west side of the lake, there was a line, a straight line.

He saw it and didn't see it, looked away and kept walking, thinking of the skis, and then stopped, did a long double take and looked again and there it was—a straight line in the snow across the lake.

Brian had discovered that there are almost no straight lines in nature. The sides of trees up and down, the horizon far away, but very little else. Animal tracks almost always wandered, circled; seldom did they go straight for any distance.

But the lake was a mile away. The line could be anything. He walked closer, watching it as he came off the ridge until the trees blotted it out and then picking up the pace, sliding the snowshoes over the hard surface as fast as he could move until he saw it again—not on the lake, this time, but through the trees ahead before going out onto the ice.

The same line.

Closer, he could see that it was not just a line but a depression in the snow that went along straight and when he moved still closer he could see that the depression was about five inches deep, almost two feet wide, and the bottom of it was as smooth as packed ice; a flattened trail that went off the bank and out on the surface of the lake.

It was most definitely not a natural trail. Something had come along here. There were no tracks, just the smooth, flat, wide depression, and Brian squatted by the side of it and tried to visualize what had made this path.

Something came by here, he thought, and then no, not something but *somebody* came by here.

A person.

Ahh, he thought—another person in the world. He had come to think there were no other people and here was this strange track. Almost certainly a person made it but in what manner . . .

Then he saw the edge of a print. On the side of the flattened area, just to the edge, was one clear wolf print. It was as plain as if the wolf had stepped in plaster and made a cast; in the soft snow from the warm weather there was a wolf print. One. Heading out on the lake.

Somebody with a wolf?

No, that didn't work. Somebody walking, pulling something, and then coming on an old wolf trail and covering the tracks, all but one.

Pulling what—a toboggan of some kind? Somebody coming along pulling a toboggan on an old wolf trail out here in the middle of the wilderness?

Out *here*?

It was insane. Brian wasn't sure where he was, had no true idea how far the plane had come off course before he crashed, but he was certain nobody could have pulled a toboggan from civilization out here and for a second he doubted that he was seeing what he was actually seeing—a track left by a person. Perhaps he was hallucinating.

But he shook his head and it was still there, all of it, and if he was dreaming this or hallucinating it then he would have to have hallucinated all of it, the wolves, the moose kill, the popping sounds . . .

No. It was real.

So what did he do?

Follow the tracks, he thought—don't be stupid.

But which way? There was no indication from the flat surface of the track of any direction. Just the wolf print, heading out onto the lake.

Well, why not? That way was as good as any and Brian set off, walking on the track itself, which was like a packed highway. If he was not particularly excited, it was because in truth some part of him did not believe what he was seeing, what he was doing.

He crossed the lake and went into the woods on the other side and there was no change, just the hard-packed trail out ahead of him, and he kept moving, seeing the wolf prints more often, especially where the trail curved around a tree—the prints would be on the outside—and in this way he passed the day.

Toward midafternoon he was hungry and stopped to eat from the meat in his pouch, eating snow to wash it down, and then he set off again and just before dark he caught a smell he knew well.

Smoke. Just a taint on the faint breeze that had come up. Some of the dry dead wood and a bit of pine, he thought, sniffing, and then it was gone, and he kept walking, thinking he must be close now, or the wind had carried it far and in the evening light he came around a corner past a large evergreen and was facing four wolves.

Except they weren't. They looked like wolves at first, large, slab-sided gray beasts in the dim light, but then he saw they were tied, their chains leading back to trees. They were watching him come and wagging their tails, and he knew they were dogs.

Four huge malamutes.

The one on the left whined softly and wiggled, trying to get him to come and pet, and Brian stood there, stunned, when beyond the dogs he saw a crude log shelter covered with brush and a skin door. As he looked, a Native American man with a rifle stepped out of the door, saw Brian and nodded.

"It's you—I wondered when you'd come by."

Brian stood, his mouth open.

"We've got beaver cooking here, plenty for all of us."

"I . . .

"But how . . . why . . . who?"

"Smelled your smoke three weeks ago. I didn't want to bother you—there's some in the bush want to be alone. Figured you'd be here before this but come on in . . ." He turned and said something back into the shelter and two small children came out and stood next to the man and a woman looked out over his shoulder.

"I . . . don't know what to say." And Brian knew he meant it. He hadn't spoken to a person in . . . he had to stop and think. The days weren't there anymore—always they had been there in the back of his mind, every day, the count, and now they were gone.

The man disappeared back inside the hut and Brian still stood, the dogs whining softly, wiggling to be petted, and in a minute the man's head popped back out.

"Are you coming inside?"

"I . . . ," Brian started, then stopped and kicked out of his snowshoes and walked inside the hut.

───── EPILOGUE ─────

They were a Cree trapping family and they had worked this area for three years. As soon as the ice was frozen on the lakes they flew in by bushplane and set up camp, trapping beaver, fox, coyote, marten, fisher and some lynx, living on moose meat—the popping sounds Brian had heard were the man, named David Smallhorn, shooting a moose for camp meat—and supplies brought in by air.

The plane came back every six weeks, bringing more fuel and staples—flour, rice and potatoes—and school supplies for the home schooling of the two children. Brian stayed with them for three weeks until the plane returned with the next load.

The Smallhorn family were scrupulously polite and because they had lived in the bush and didn't have television, they knew nothing of Brian's disaster. They thought he must be another trapper. It wasn't until after they'd eaten beaver meat broiled over a small metal stove in the log hut that David leaned over and asked:

"How come is it you have skins for clothes and stone arrowheads? You look like one of the old-way people . . ."

And Brian explained how he came to be in the woods, talking about each day as it had come, as he could remember it, until it was late and the children's heads were bobbing with sleep and finally David held up his hand.

"Tomorrow. More tomorrow. We'll take the dogs and toboggan and go back to your camp, bring your things here, and then you can tell us more and show me how to shoot that thing"—he pointed to the bow—"and how to make arrowheads." He smiled. "We don't use them anymore . . ."

And Brian slept in his clothes that night in the hut with the Smallhorns and the next day watched while David harnessed the dogs and they set off on snowshoes. The dogs followed behind, pulling the toboggan, and in one trip they brought back all that Brian owned, including the meat supply. Brian sat another evening and night telling them of all the things he had done and become. He showed them the bows and fish spears and killing lance while they ate boiled potatoes and moose hump and had coffee thick with sugar, and the next morning Brian went with David on his trapline. They walked on snowshoes while the dogs followed, pulling the toboggan, to load dead beaver from trap-sets, and it came to be that within a week Brian was almost part of the family, and within two weeks he had to force himself to remember living alone and surviving. By the third week, when he watched the bushplane circle and land on the lake ice on skis, the truth was he almost didn't want to leave. The woods had become so much a part of his life—the heat of it seemed to match his pulse, his breathing—that as he helped the Smallhorns and pilot unload, he felt as if he were unloading gear and food for himself, as well as the family; as though he would be staying to watch the plane leave.

But when it was done and everything unloaded, the pilot looked at him and nodded to the sky. "There's weather coming in—I want to be gone before it hits . . ." Brian stood by the plane, his hand on the wing strut, looking at the Smallhorns, who were standing by the pile of supplies.

In the long hours of darkness, they had sipped tea and eaten greasy beaver meat and talked, and David knew Brian enough to know why he hesitated. He left the pile of supplies and came forward and smiled and waved an arm around at the country, all the country, all the woods and lakes and sky and all that was in it. He knew, and he touched Brian on the shoulder and said:

"It will be here when you come back. We'll keep the soup hot . . ."

And Brian turned and stepped up into the plane.

About the Author

Gary Paulsen is the distinguished author of many critically acclaimed books for young people, including three Newbery Honor books: *The Winter Room*, *Hatchet* and *Dogsong*. His novel *The Haymeadow* received the Western Writers of America Golden Spur Award. His newest books are *Nightjohn*, *Mr. Tucket*, *Call Me Francis Tucket*, and *Father Water, Mother Woods: Essays on Fishing and Hunting in the North Woods*. He and his wife have homes in New Mexico and on the Pacific.